A LITTLE GAME CALLED MURDER

By Emberlyn Grace

Printed in the United States of America
Print ISBN: 9781951490744
E-Book ISBN: 9781951490751

Canoe Tree
Press

4697 Main Street
Manchester Center, VT 05255
Canoe Tree Press is a division of DartFrog Books.

Special thanks to my family for putting up
with my insane schedule as I wrote this book
and pushing me to reach for my goals. And
to my supportive friends, Michaela, Alyce,
Ellsie, and Grasha, who inspired me and
stood by me through the entire journey.

PROLOGUE

Welcome to Ashland, Oregon. Nestled in the foothills of the Cascades just sixteen miles north of the border with California. A quiet little town with the rich tapestry of nature all around. The perfect place to enjoy wineries, the arts, and so much more.

But hidden in this natural paradise, a secret lurks. One that will soon grip the area with fear. And death...

CHAPTER ONE

Tuesday, October 8, 2019
8:45 a.m.

"911, what is your emergency?"

"I—I—oh God..."

From the other end of the line, the dispatcher could hear the sobs wracking the woman's body. Her voice cracked as she quietly continued.

"I... I found a body."

"Can you repeat that, please?" he asked, unsure if he had heard her correctly.

"I found a body... "

"You found a body?"

"Yes... oh God, it's so awful... "

Taking a deep breath to calm his own voice, Brian Sands prepared for what would soon become a horrific turn of events. "Is the person still breathing?" *Get her to give the details, then move on, Brian. She's traumatized enough.*

"No... she's dead... and there's so much blood," the woman cried.

"Okay, what's your name, ma'am?"

"It's Zoey... Zoey Bonnall."

"All right, Zoey, my name is Brian. Zoey, can you tell me where you are?"

Sniffling, Zoey replied, "I'm on the Pacific Crest Trail."

"Zoey, it's going to be all right. I'm dispatching officers to your location now," Brian answered.

"Thank you, Brian."

"Just stay on the line with me, Zoey. Help is on the way..."

An hour after Brian fielded the terrified call from Zoey, rookie cop Sarah Lawson stood on the wooded trail with a still-sobbing Zoey and another officer. Twenty yards from them lay the bloodied body of the victim, while medical examiner Blake Sheldon and his team stood around her, making notes. Coming up the trail were crime scene technicians, prepared to photograph and collect evidence once the medical examiner and the detectives gave the green light.

The dappled light streaming through the limbs of the trees bathed them in an eerily pale glow. Sarah looked with compassion at the woman beside her in her athletic clothes, tears long having soaked through her purple top. Glancing at the other officer, Sarah cleared her throat and addressed the witness.

"Zoey, it's going to be all right now."

"I... I know, but... God, I never expected to find a dead body on my morning run."

Officer Morrigan Hammons, a freckle-faced young woman, placed a gentle hand on Zoey's shoulder while Sarah continued. "Officer Hammons can take you home now, but the detectives for the case will need to speak to you soon," Sarah told her.

"I understand. Thank you, Officer Lawson."

With a long face, Zoey allowed Officer Hammons to lead her away from the bloody scene. Sarah peered across the clearing at the M.E., not sure of her next move. After all, this was her first true crime scene since graduating from the police academy.

"Dr. Sheldon, everything okay?" she called.

The white-haired doctor looked over at her, his dark blue eyes distant behind his black glasses. With exhaustion etched upon his face, he rubbed his temples before answering. "Yeah, but you better get Cortenza and Stevens out here, kid."

Kid... really? Sarah rolled her eyes at the nickname, but already was reaching for her phone. "On it!" Looking at her phone, she pulled up her contacts, searching for the recently added numbers. *Okay, who do I call first? I've heard Cortenza doesn't usually answer, so maybe I'll try Audrey Stevens first.* Hitting the button, she waited in anticipation as it rang.

"Hello?"

"Detective Stevens, this is Officer Lawson. I'm calling because we have a homicide off Pacific Coast Trail."

Sarah heard the swift intake of air followed by a soft sigh through the phone. "Okay, thanks for calling. I'll be there in forty-five, and I'll grab Vince on my way. Although, chances are I'll be dragging his ass out of bed and making awkward eyes with his latest lay in the process. So... better make it an hour."

"Thanks, Detective," Sarah responded, stifling her giggles at the image the other woman had put in her head. Hanging up, she shook her head to dispel the impure thoughts. Vince Cortenza might be an attractive Italian-American player, but she still had a dead body only feet away. *Definitely not the time or place, girl.*

Inside a black and glass minimalist-style home, Audrey Stevens hung up her phone and turned to look thoughtfully at her husband, Declan. She brushed her long blonde hair from her shoulder, her blue eyes reflecting the light pouring in from their windowed ceiling. Declan's own brown hair was messy and tousled from sleep, his broad tanned chest sporting the tattoo she loved to trace.

"Problem, baby?"

"That was the new girl," she answered, tossing her phone back on the unmade bed. "Apparently there's been a homicide."

Concern lit on Declan's features as he took in the slumped shoulders of his wife. "Oh, that's terrible, Audrey. Isn't that the second homicide in the past month?"

"Yep. Two in the past two weeks actually. It's highly unusual for a little town like Ashland, but my days of quietly being a detective may be coming to an end," she sighed.

"Well, we have been getting a bunch of tourists from Cali lately," Declan mused. "And you know what they say, babe."

"What's that, Declan?

"That one friend out of every group has the potential to be a serial killer," he said with a hearty laugh.

Audrey looked less amused, crossing her arms over her chest. Giving her husband a look of disapproval, she shook her head. "I'll be sure to tell that one to Vince. I'd bet he'll find that funny. Now, I've got to get changed, Dec." She pushed past him on her way to the bathroom.

"I love you," he called after her.

Over the sound of the shower coming to life, she quipped, "Oh, I know."

Back on the trail, crime scene technicians and paramedics were staying busy as they waited for the two detectives. One tech, Denise, was gossiping with Sarah as Audrey and Vince walked up the path. Waving in greeting, Denise smiled at Audrey, knowing today would hit her hard.

"Audrey, you look good today."

"Hey, Denise. Likewise," Audrey returned. "Lawson, nice to see you."

Before the rookie could mutter a reply, Denise

catcalled the tall man approaching. "Woo, somebody call the fire department! It just got a hell of a lot hotter here," she said.

Vince winked cheekily in her direction, Sarah looking woefully uncomfortable and Audrey rolling her eyes.

"Simmer down, D. Last time I checked, this was still a crime scene," Audrey reminded her.

"You're right, Audrey. Sorry."

"No need to apologize, babe," Vince crooned. "I know I'm irresistible."

"Okay... so..." Sarah attempted, looking between the three in confusion.

"Let's start with the vic's name, Lawson," Audrey offered.

"Yes... right!" *Keep it together, Sarah! You want to be a detective one day, remember!* She scolded herself for her unprofessionalism as she pulled her notepad from her pocket. "So, the victim is twenty-nine years old, and according to the ID in her pocket, her name is Kristy Hillman—"

"Kristy?" Audrey shrieked, cutting her off mid-sentence. "There's got to be a mistake. I saw her last Friday at our book club!"

Denise shared a sympathetic glance with Sarah and Vince, her lavender eyes bright. "Sorry, Audrey, but it's her."

"Oh God, Audrey," Vince breathed, "are you okay?" They all watched as her face seemed to turn green and tears filled her eyes.

"I... I need a minute..." she whispered, turning away from them before running off a short distance.

Vince's brown eyes were fixed on the fallen leaves, a weary look distorting his usually handsome features. Rubbing a hand across the stubble on his jaw, he looked at Denise in despair. "Damn, this is going to hit her hard."

"What do you mean, Cortenza?" Sarah asked.

"You're telling me you don't know, Sarah?" Denise asked in surprise.

Sarah rubbed her arm nervously, afraid she had missed something huge. She pushed her curly brown hair out of her face and looked between Denise and Vince as she shifted her weight repeatedly. Shaking her head, she waited in anticipation for the bombshell.

"Last week we found the body of another of Audrey's friends—"

"Monica, right?" Denise interrupted.

Nodding, Vince confirmed the identity for her.

"You two dated, didn't you?"

"Well, hooked up is probably a more apt description of our relationship, D."

"One-night stands are about as far as you usually get, Vince," Denise quipped.

"Hey, I prefer to think of them as trial marriages with far less money and commitment involved, honey," Vince defended.

Batting her lashes, Denise purred back at him, clearly hoping for a good time later. "Anytime you wanna 'marry me,' you've got my number."

Sarah shifted uncomfortably, feeling like she was caught between two horny teenagers. Vince was eying Denise's curvy figure like a ravenous wolf. Sarah tried to block the heat crawling up her face by listening to the rustle of the leaves and the calling of birds, but to no avail.

"Um... is it appropriate to be talking about sex right now?" Sarah asked nervously.

"Hey, sex makes the world go 'round, Sarah," Vince replied with a seductive wink.

"You can make me go 'round, Vince," Denise giggled.

"Seriously, guys. Her body is twenty feet away."

"Relax, Lawson," Vince told her. "Kristy was a sex kitten. Believe me, she wouldn't mind this conversation in the slightest."

"He's right," Denise reassured her. "And look, I know I came off like a slut when this one walked up," she nodded her head at Vince, "especially since Kristy and Stevens were friends, but let's be real for a minute. As horribly sad as her death is, we are all still alive, kicking, and have needs. Sex is one of the easiest ways to feel alive, Sarah."

Mercifully, Audrey was rejoining their group, so the sex-talk was tabled quickly. The blonde-haired detective seemed to trudge her way back to them, her eyes looking devoid of life. Sarah rubbed her arm to calm her nerves, uncertain how to reestablish the conversation with the veteran officer after the hit she had just sustained.

Fortunately, Vince gently broke the ice, placing a hand lightly on her shoulder. "Audrey, are you okay?"

She took a deep breath before responding, her glazed eyes staring sightlessly at the leaf-littered forest path. "I'll be fine," she said quietly.

"Girl, I'm sure we can get another detective—" Denise started.

"I said I'll be fine, Denise," Audrey snapped. Seeing the shock on the tech's face, Audrey's softened. "Kristy is—was—my friend. I owe it to her to find the truth."

Vince watched her closely for a moment, his dark brows knit together in concentration. He crossed his muscular arms over his chest, looking down slightly at her bowed golden head. "Audrey, you said that last week about Monica, too."

Facing him with a sudden fire in her eyes, Audrey raised her chin as high as she could manage. "And I meant it both times, Vincent. Drop it." She swiveled her body toward the other women and saw the concern etched on their faces. "Honestly, guys, I'll be doing better if I'm here helping."

"Okay, but the second it becomes too much, let me know," Vince told her with a shrug.

"I promise."

Everyone in the foursome exhaled the breaths they hadn't realized they were holding, knowing the issue had been temporarily resolved. Sarah looked around the group, not completely certain what the next step should be for them. Clearing her throat and drawing the dark blue eyes of Audrey, she squeaked, "So... what do we do now?"

"First things first, we talk with the medical examiner, Lawson," Audrey answered her.

Vince put his hands up in protest, having glimpsed the body already and knowing the report was not going to be pretty. "Audrey, I'll talk to Blake and the paramedics."

"Sounds good, Cortenza," she said, watching with exhaustion as he stepped beyond them to speak privately. "Rookie, that means you're with Denise and me on evidence collection."

As Sarah gulped nervously, Denise looked around the crime scene. "Henry is here somewhere, and Cathy answered the call with Josh in the ambulance."

Audrey's keen eyes scanned the area as well, noting Dr. Sheldon was in deep conversation with Vince, yet the other three people were missing. "They may have gone to get the stretcher and body bag for Blake."

"Probably true," Denise returned, a mischievous glint in her eye. "You better hope that's all they're doing."

"You're bad, D," Audrey managed, a smile briefly lighting her face. It disappeared when she peered beyond Sarah's shoulder and saw the bloodied remains of her friend.

"All right, Lawson, you ready to get your feet wet?" Denise asked.

"Yeah... sure," Sarah said, her face going pale.

"Follow us, then."

Approaching the body itself was horrific. Kristy's dark blonde hair was matted with sticky crimson spray, as were her shredded clothes. A pool of blood was beneath her, darkening the leaves and dying grass almost black. Bruises were visible on her tanned skin, and her left arm looked broken.

"She looks like a paper doll that was ripped to shreds," Audrey whispered.

Denise wrapped a comforting arm around her, providing warmth as a sudden gust blew past them. Leaning close, she rested her forehead against Audrey's, hoping to encourage her friend. "Just take it one step at a time, girl."

Nodding and brushing the moisture from her eyes, Audrey turned to Sarah. "Okay, Sarah, first we need to take photographs of the scene and body."

Sarah grabbed the camera for Denise who flicked the switch to turn it on. She swallowed hard at the bile rising in her throat, determined that if Audrey could handle it, so could she. Sarah got closer to the body, ready to hand rulers to Denise as she needed them.

"We start with the whole body and scene," Denise told her. "I focus the camera at her stomach since that is the epicenter of the scene."

Denise began clicking away, snapping the photos that would hopefully lead them to Kristy Hillman's killer. After the initial shots were completed, she photographed Kristy's brutally bruised and cut face, her extended left arm bent at an unnatural angle, the extreme blood splatter on her pants, and finally, her bare feet.

Squinting, Audrey leaned closer to the body, trying to get a better view of something lodged partially under Kristy. "Denise, do you see that?"

Denise squatted down and her purple eyes widened in surprise. "I do, A. What the hell is it, though? Let me get a shot of the top of her jeans and I'll zoom way in, okay?" Denise told her, laying a ruler in the blood.

Sarah took the picture, then all three stood to look at the camera. "I'll be damned," Denise whispered, "there's a pair of frickin' dice under her."

"That's the weirdest thing I've ever seen before," Sarah commented.

Denise glanced over at the young woman and chuckled. "You should ride with me more often, honey. Oh, the stories I could tell you..." she trailed off with a sigh.

"Focus, Denise," Audrey murmured. "We are still on the job here. That should just about wrap up this part, Lawson."

Sarah returned the camera to the carrier while Denise carefully transferred the bloody dice to an evidence bag. As Denise stared at the odd markings, her mind was flashing a code of information she couldn't comprehend. *There's something familiar about these dice,* she thought.

Shaking her head to dispel her wandering thoughts, Denise tucked the evidence bag into the kit already full of samples from the surrounding crime scene. "I'll get these to trace, and I'll have the evidence sheet for you in an hour or two," she said as she hoisted the kit off the ground.

"Come on, Lawson, you can ride with Henry and me," Denise said with a tilt of her dark head. "Audrey, call me if you need me, babe."

Audrey observed as the many people in attendance began to disperse. First, it was Sarah and Denise, who were joined by a ginger-haired young man. Then, Dr. Sheldon and his crew carefully steered the stretcher laden with the black body bag. Feeling sadness threatening to creep upon her the longer she watched, Audrey withdrew and met Vince as he headed her way. His notebook in his hand and a worried expression on his face, she thought it was evident whatever Blake had told her partner had been brutal.

"What did Blake say?" Audrey asked timidly.

Vince tucked his notepad in the breast pocket of his uniform and looked thoughtfully at his partner. "Do you really want to know?"

"Vince, just tell me. I'm going to find out sooner or later," Audrey said, crossing her arms impatiently over her chest.

"It isn't pretty, Drey. It looks like she was stabbed upwards of ten times, just from his cursory exam," he started.

Audrey's face went ashen at his words, and her hands clutched before her heart. "Ten times? Oh my God," she breathed.

"I told you that you didn't want to know."

"Vince, saying 'I told you so' doesn't help right now," Audrey snapped.

"You're right, I'm sorry. But God, Drey, I don't know why you're putting yourself through this."

"Because she was a friend, Vince! And it's my fucking job! So, let me do it!" she screamed.

Vince quickly pulled her into a tight hug, rubbing her back soothingly to calm her. Audrey sniffed loudly into his shirt, gently banging her head against his chest.

"Okay... okay, Audrey. It's going to be all right. I get it... really, I do. I'll give you the rest of Blake's report later, but for now, let's head back to the precinct, okay?"

Stepping out of his embrace and swiping at her face, Audrey nodded miserably. "Fine, Vince." As she headed down the path toward their car, she called over her shoulder, "But you're driving."

Thirty minutes later, the pair were walking into the downtown precinct. A couple officers were milling about the lobby, talking quietly as they entered. The secretary scurried toward the chief's office and disappeared inside as Audrey stopped to get a cup of coffee.

"Do we have the contact info for the witness?" she asked as she blew on the hot drink.

"I don't, but I can get it from Brian," Vince told her, taking the coffee pot from her to fill his own cup. "Blake said he was the one who took the call this morning."

"Brian is a good egg," Audrey smiled. "He's one of the best I've seen at keeping people calm when they call."

"He really is," Vince agreed, grimacing at the coffee in his hand. "Who the hell made this crap? It tastes like tar."

Audrey giggled, feeling lighter than she had all morning at his comment. That brief exchange quickly deflated as the secretary rushed back to her desk, and their chief, Shawn Mitchel exited his office. All eyes were instantly drawn to his face, as his hazel gaze found Audrey.

"Stevens, a word?" he said in his gravelly voice.

Handing her cup to Vince, she nodded. "Sure, Chief."

"I'll get that info from Brian and meet you in the bullpen," Vince told her as she started following Mitchel to his office. "And I'm sending someone to get better coffee."

Glowering at their secretary, Vince poured their coffees down the drain and marched out of the lobby. The other two officers still present looked at each other hesitantly, unsure of the coming events. Morrigan Hammons, the officer who had responded with Sarah to the scene, worried her lower lip as she glanced at the chief's office door.

"What do you suppose that's all about?" she asked Roger sheepishly.

Beside her, Roger Anderson ran a hand through his curly brown hair and shrugged. "My guess is the chief will try to take Stevens off the case."

"You don't really think that, do you?" Morrigan asked.

"Why not, Morri? She has a personal connection to the vic. It makes sense."

"But she's one of our best detectives, Roger."

"We'll just have to wait and see."

———•———

Inside the office, Audrey had shut the door as instructed and waited anxiously for Chief Mitchel to speak. After a full minute of silence as he simply stood and evaluated her with his eyes, she broke the tension by asking, "Am I in trouble?"

Sighing, Shawn sat at his desk and motioned for her to take the seat before it. "Stevens, I've known you for a long time," he started. "You were the one to introduce me and Shannon. I also know how tenacious—make that stubborn as a mule—you can be at times."

Audrey managed a thin-lipped smile at his description of her. She nodded slightly, hoping he would continue.

"I just want to see how you're holding up. Two of your friends have been found dead in the past two weeks, Audrey. That can't be easy on you."

"I won't lie to you, Shawn, when I got to the scene this morning and they told me it was Kristy," Audrey paused, taking a deep breath. "For a moment I couldn't breathe. I stepped away to compose myself."

"Oh, Audrey," Shawn whispered.

"In all honesty, I feel numb, Shawn."

Rising from his desk to pace in frustration, he looked at her hard. "Then let me call in another detective from Medford. You don't need to do this!'"

"No... I may be numb now, but later... later I'll feel the sorrow and regret." She looked down at her hands, clasped tightly in her lap. When she raised her head to look at him again, tears shone in her brilliant blue eyes. "I know if I don't help find what happened to my friends... Shawn, a part of me will always blame myself."

"Okay, fine, Audrey," he said, pinching the bridge of his nose like he was getting a headache. "But if this becomes too much—"

"I promise I'll let you and Vince know," she finished for him, standing to her feet.

"Fair enough, I suppose," Shawn said, nodding. "Keep Lawson with you for this case since she wants to be a detective. She may as well learn from the best and that's you and Cortenza."

"Sure thing, chief. And thanks for understanding, Shawn," Audrey said quietly.

Pointing a finger at her with a serious look marking his face, Shawn sat back down in his chair. "Don't make me regret it, all right?"

"I'll do my best," she promised, before walking to the door.

———•———

Out in the bullpen, officers typed furiously on computers, shuffled papers into file folders, or compared notes with one another over various cases. Audrey made her way over to the desks she and Vince Cortenza called home, watching his well-formed hands flip through a small stack of papers.

"Get anything interesting?" she asked, causing him to jump.

"Geez, walk a little louder next time, Drey. You trying to give me a heart attack?"

"Get over it, you big baby," Audrey snickered, enjoying the look of annoyance that crossed his face. "I repeat, did you learn anything interesting?"

"On the witness, or Kristy?"

"Either."

"Witness's name is Zoey Bonnall. According to what Brian gave me, she works at a local gym in administration."

"So, she's a paper-pusher?" Audrey asked.

Vince shrugged, but a coy smile curved his lips upward. "Basically, but I heard she's got a smokin' body."

Audrey rolled her eyes. *Some things never change.*

Vince will always be a player. "Keep it in your pants, Vince."

"I'll try, Drey," he said with a chuckle. "Brian is printing up the 911 recording and should be bringing that up soon."

"Okay, sounds like a good start with her, then; how about with Kristy?"

Rubbing the back of his neck, his brown eyes held worry. "That's where things start to not add up, honestly."

"How so?" she asked, surprised.

"You and the rest of your book club girls saw her last Friday, right?"

"Yeah, that's right," Audrey confirmed. "We met the same time, same place as always, got out the same time, and went home."

"That's four days ago, Drey. I mean, I know Kristy was a bit of a bed-hopper, but four days is a long enough time that someone should have noticed and reported her missing."

They both paused and looked at one another, thoughts swirling in their minds. Audrey counted the days herself, wondering how Kristy's disappearance could have gone unnoticed. Unless...

"It's Tuesday..." she started, looking pensive.

"What are you thinking?"

"Kristy was the head cheer coach at the high school, Vince. I wonder if she called in sick yesterday or today."

Vince motioned to the stack of papers on his desk.

"I've already got the school on my list of contacts."

"I guess we should go look at her apartment, too, huh?" Audrey said, unease filling her.

"Yeah, standard procedure and all. Plus, maybe one of her neighbors saw something," he added as he picked up a file that had fallen with the slamming of a door. "People, breezes destroy organization," he muttered. His eyes fell on the text, and a light bulb seemed to illuminate his mind.

"This is interesting, Drey. Both Monica and Kristy live at the same apartment complex."

"Yeah, Hampton Meadows," she answered, unimpressed. She caught the look on his face; she could practically see the wheels turning in his head. "You think it's connected?"

"More than them both being in the same book club? I'm not sure, but it seems like one hell of a coincidence," Vince stated. "Two single girls, living in the same complex, in the same book club, dying within days of each other?"

"Creepy as hell, yes," Audrey agreed. "Coincidence? Maybe. Does it make me not want to rent an apartment there and quit my book club? Possibly. But let's get some facts first."

Cortenza studied her briefly. "You mean you didn't know?"

"Didn't know what, Vince?"

"I had completely forgotten about it until now, but..." he began before trailing off, his hand rubbing his chin thoughtfully.

After a moment of silence, Audrey felt her impatience growing. "Are you going to confide in me, or just stand there?" Oblivious to her comment, Vince continued to stand in relative silence, slight mutterings escaping his mouth from time to time. Waving her hand in front of his face, Audrey nearly yelled his name. "Vincent Adrianno Cortenza!'"

Startled, he shook his head in disbelief before crossing his arms angrily over his chest. "Hey! Why are you middle-naming me?"

"Maybe if you wouldn't go into a trance like that, I wouldn't," Audrey fired back, hands firmly on her hips.

Vince rolled his eyes in annoyance. "Sorry, I was just refreshing my memory.'"

"And have you finished taking baking soda to your brain, Vincey?"

"Sheesh, yes. And don't call me Vincey," he growled. "Anyway, about six months ago, Kristy and I hooked up—"

"Spare me the details!" Audrey cried, visibly cringing.

"—and she mentioned her landlord had been acting..." he paused to think, "'more interested than usual', I think is how she put it."

"And since they had the same landlord..."

". . . he just became person of interest number one on the list," he finished.

Sarah came walking up, a file in her hand from Denise. Hesitantly, she approached the detectives, waving in greeting.

"Hey, Sarah," Audrey replied.

"Whatcha got there, sweetness?" Vince asked flirtatiously.

Sarah blushed to her roots and failed miserably to recover. "It's... um... the log," she began, her face heating further as she found Cortenza's eyes on her. "Of evidence!" she quickly added. Thrusting the file to Audrey, she rushed to correct herself: "It's the evidence log from today."

Vince snickered while Audrey rolled her eyes. She shared a slight wink with Lawson before opening the file. "Just ignore him, Sarah. He's a toddler."

"Were you aware that today's vic and Monica Simpson were neighbors?" Sarah asked.

"Yeah, we just established that," Vince nodded.

"Oh," Sarah squeaked, "then you probably already made the connection.'"

"What connection?" Audrey asked, not taking her eyes from the report. "About their landlord?"

"I don't know anything about a landlord," Sarah voiced, "but I thought you had noticed the dice in both cases."

Audrey's head snapped up and the report slipped from her hands as Vince asked, "What dice?"

CHAPTER TWO

Sarah looked between the two detectives and rubbed her arm. "Well, we found a pair of dice under Ms. Hillman's body today. Then Denise found the report from last week and apparently there were the same dice found at the last scene as well."

"You mean to tell me there were dice at both locations?" Audrey asked, clearly shocked.

"Damn," Vince breathed, "it sounds like we may have a serial killer on our hands. I'm assuming the dice aren't part of the book club, right?"

Audrey turned to face her partner, a look of disgusted annoyance on her face. "No, Vince. We're a book club. We don't do D-and-D."

"Okay, okay! Just checking!"

"Lawson, you're positive they're the same type of dice?" Audrey questioned, turning again to the rookie cop.

"Yes, ma'am. They're the same. Apparently, one has symbols on it and the other has words."

"What type of words are we talking about here, Sarah?" Vince asked, rubbing his jaw thoughtfully. Other officers buzzed around them, oblivious to the potentially serious nature of their discussion. The three moved closer together to keep the conversation more private.

Audrey perused the report herself, flipping through the black and white images printed on the papers. "According to the report," she began, "looks like *die, sterben, hiltzen, mourir, bās,* and *morire.*"

"Do you think they all mean 'dice'?" Sarah asked.

"Definitely not," Vince replied.

Both women turned to regard him with curiosity. Audrey cleared her throat as she laid the report on her desk. "What makes you say that, Vince?"

"Well, I happen to know *morire* is Italian for 'die.' As in death."

"How do you know that, Cortenza?" Sarah asked, enamored.

"Are you kidding me, Lawson? My *nonna* would be rolling in her grave if I hadn't learned Italian," he answered with a chuckle.

"Declan's family hail from Ireland," Audrey said, thinking aloud. "I'm pretty sure *bās* is Irish for 'die.' And if that's the case, I think it would be safe to assume the others mean the same."

Taking a deep breath, Vince's brown eyes settled gloomily on Audrey's face. "Fair assessment, Drey, but I think you're forgetting something." Her deep blue orbs swiveled to look at him, questions sparking like fireworks in their depths. Raising a blonde brow, she waited for him to continue. "The M.O. doesn't match," he said.

"True. Kristy was clearly stabbed, but Monica drowned," she replied.

Sarah nervously interjected, "But what about the markings on the second die?"

Audrey again picked up the report, Vince peering over her shoulder as she read. "Looks like there are six different symbols. A noose, a shovel, a gun, the poison symbol, a knife, and squiggly lines."

"Those squiggly lines could mean water, right?" Vince noted. "I mean, that would make sense."

"So those symbols could represent the cause of death!" Sarah exclaimed.

Nodding, Vince answered her approvingly. "So, it would seem, Lawson."

"But that means..." Sarah trailed, not wanting to voice her concern. Audrey finished for her, resignation in her voice.

"It means that we may be looking at four more targets."

"This is not good, ladies."

"I agree," Audrey said, "so let's get our asses in gear. Vince, where do you want to go first: the school or her apartment?"

"Are we taking Lawson here with us?"

"Actually, if you're okay with this, Sarah, I'd like you to head to the lab to stay on top of Denise's team. If we do in fact have a serial killer on the loose, time is of the essence. You being at the lab to relay info could be what breaks the case," Audrey told her.

Pride swelled in Sarah's chest, tinged with just a hint of disappointment. Although she longed to join them in the field to question potential witnesses, she felt excited to know Audrey and Vince would trust her to be their eyes and ears at the lab. "I can do that, detective," she said quietly.

"Good deal. Call us if you learn anything vital," Audrey said dismissively.

Sarah hurried to grab her jacket and keys, eager to please the senior officers. Audrey turned her full attention back to Vince, who was already grabbing the keys to their car and his notebook. "All right, Vince, where to first?"

"How about we head to the school, Drey? Question them before they let out for the day?"

"Sounds like a plan, Vince."

⸺ ◆ ⸺

Twenty minutes later, the two were walking the quiet halls of the high school. Vince glanced down at his partner, noting her eyes were vacant. "I spoke to the principal, and he said he'd meet us in the gym."

Audrey paused briefly to look up him, her eyes clouded with questions. "In the gym? What the hell? What not his office?"

Shrugging, Vince answered, "Search me, Stevens. I don't know. Maybe because she was the cheer coach and that's where her office is. Let's just get in there and get it over with."

At the entrance to the locker area, Principal Milton Howard, a stocky little man with a deeply receding hair line, waited impatiently for them. Pushing his thick glasses farther up his nose, he motioned for them to follow him inside. Audrey rolled her eyes as she and Vince walked in silence after the eccentric principal.

"... our assistant coach is here as well," he told them as they entered the weight room. Howard had been rambling for the past two minutes about the cheer team, seemingly oblivious to the gravity of the entire situation. The assistant coach looked in their direction at the commotion, her ash-blonde hair framing her pale face and hazel eyes.

"Milton?" she queried, ignoring the two girls behind her.

"Phyllis, these are Detectives Cortenna and Stevens—" he stated.

"Cortenza, actually, sir," he corrected.

Principal Howard faced him and eyed him up and down before shrugging and turning back to the woman in front of him. "Right, whatever. They have some questions relating to Kristy. If you need me, I'll be in my office."

As the man left, the two high-schoolers blushed as they took in Vince's physique. One looking very much like the stereotypical cheerleader with her tanned skin, blonde hair in pigtails, and pink ensemble, and the other more reserved and athletic-looking, her chocolate-brown skin dotted with beads of perspiration, her red-dyed hair loose around her face.

"Oh em gee," the blonde chirped. "Did something, like, happen to Coach Hillman?"

Audrey rolled her eyes at the girl's inappropriateness but bit her tongue. The other cheerleader jabbed her in the ribs with her elbow. "Rachel, hush!"

"Brittany, that freaking hurt!" Rachel wailed.

Ignoring them, Vince turned his attention to Phyllis Whitmore. "Did she call in sick yesterday or today?"

"Ha, keep dreaming, officer," Phyllis answered. "The day Kristy Hillman thinks of anyone other than herself will be the day pigs fly. Don't tell me, she ran off with some loser bum, am I right?"

"Actually, she's dead, so try to show a little respect," Audrey hissed.

Vince turned to place a hand on her shoulder, warning her to cool down. Brittany's voice chimed softly behind them, "Dead? No way..."

"Oh my gosh, this is terrible," Rachel exclaimed. "She wasn't wearing anything expensive when she died, was she?"

Vince physically restrained Audrey from launching herself at the girl as Phyllis turned to face them, arms crossed over her chest in annoyance. "Girls, I think you're done for now. Scram."

"Yes, coach," Brittany said quickly, beating a hasty retreat for the door.

Rachel remained, her arms crossed in front of her like a small girl, a flirty smile on her face. "Rachel, you too," Phyllis advised.

"I just wanted to see if the hottie had a number,"

she said, twirling a strand of hair around her finger, biting her lower lip in invitation.

Wow, no shame, Audrey thought in disgust. "Trust me, kid, he's too old for you. Now beat it."

"Fine!" Rachel pouted, stomping from the room.

Phyllis shook her head in aggravation, but not disbelief. "Sorry about her. Hormones and teenage girls, am I right? Anyway, you were saying Kristy was dead?"

"You don't seem too torn up over that news," Vince mused.

"You're kidding, right? Look, I get it's sad she's dead and all, but Kristy Hillman was a selfish party girl. She never showed up on time, she was a bad influence on the girls, as Rachel is evidence of, and she was always sleeping around," Phyllis ranted.

"Do you know what her plans this past weekend were?" Vince asked, his pen poised to jot down her answer.

"I know she's in some book club on Fridays, and honestly that information shocked the hell out of me," she said with a shrug.

"And why's that?" Audrey bristled.

Phyllis eyed her skeptically. "Because Kristy is dense as a bag of rocks. I didn't think she had two brain cells to rub together in that blonde head of hers."

"Ouch," Audrey commented.

"Just stating the facts, detective. Kristy might have had the title of head coach, but when it came down to it, I was the one who did everything," Phyllis explained.

"You know, comments like that make you sound awfully bitter," Vince told her, one eyebrow raised in suspicion.

Phyllis rolled her eyes. "I won't lie and say I'm not, but I'm not dumb enough to kill someone to get ahead."

"Do you have an alibi?"

"I was at a cheer conference all weekend. Kristy didn't want to go, so I did."

"And this can be verified?" Vince asked.

"I can drop off copies of the receipts if you'd like," Phyllis said grouchily.

"Okay, okay," Vince said, holding up his hands in surrender. "Can you think of anything else?"

Phyllis paused to think back carefully, her eyes lighting suddenly with a memory. "Kristy said something about meeting someone over the weekend."

Vince leapt at the nugget of information. "Did she happen to say who or where?"

"No, but I go the impression he might have been married. The way she talked about him... it seemed like he was off-limits. She was excited because it would be risky to meet with him."

"Okay," Audrey started, already feeling weary. "Thanks for your time."

As they turned to leave, Whitmore cleared her throat. "Detectives, I know I may have come off harsh, but I do hope you find out what happened to her." Ducking her head, she slipped out of the room.

Vince turned to look at Audrey, attempting to determine her level of fatigue. "Time to head to the apartments?"

"Yeah, looks like it," she replied, resolutely heading back to their car.

Before long they were pulling up in front of the office building of the Hampton Meadows apartments. The pool was surprisingly still uncovered, bright leaves floating on its surface. Stepping out of the car, they both paused to look at the serene row of cramped apartments.

"Seems like such a peaceful little place, huh?" Vince asked.

"Yeah, but seeing as how two of my friends lived here and are now dead..." Audrey said. Glancing around, she continued, ". . . it may also be home to a psychotic killer."

"Fair enough. Let's go question the landlord."

They walked down the little path that led to the office doors. Inside, a large wood desk occupied the back wall, a small leasing office to their right, and a wiry man stood behind the desk, clearly startled by the chime from the door.

"Good afternoon," he said, once the shock had worn off. "How can I help you?"

Vince eyed him and asked, "You the landlord?"

"Um... yes... I'm Gregory Daniels," he squeaked.

Gregory Daniels was an unimpressive man of sub-par height, slight build, and forgettable features. His pale skin gave the impression he didn't spend much time outdoors and that he'd bruise like a peach if you hit him with a feather.

"I'm Detective Cortenza, and this is my partner, Detective Stevens," Vince told him.

"Is there a problem, detectives? All my permits are up to date!"

"We aren't here about your permits, Mr. Daniels," Audrey said. "We're here regarding the deaths of two of your tenants."

Gregory's mud-colored brown eyes fell. "Yes, it was such a shame to hear about Monica last week—" he started, then looked up in shock. "Wait! Did you say two?"

"Yes sir," Vince answered. "We found the body of Kristy Hillman this morning."

"Kristy's dead?" he whispered. Within seconds, Gregory began to sob. Vince and Audrey exchanged interested looks as they watched.

"Mr. Daniels, had you noticed she was missing?" Audrey asked.

"No... no, I hadn't. This is terrible! Kristy was such a sweet girl," he cried.

"Kristy claimed months ago that you were paying quite a lot of attention to her—" Vince started.

"Is there any truth to that accusation?" Audrey finished.

Gregory Daniels looked stricken at their words, color painting his pale cheeks flame red. "I... I..."

"Mr. Daniels, you need to be honest with us now," Audrey said firmly.

"I don't know what you're talking about!" he protested.

"Why would Kristy make those types of comments, then?" Vince pushed.

"I have no idea..." Gregory said. "Am I in trouble? Do I need a lawyer?"

Taking a step closer to the desk behind which he cowered, Audrey looked him dead in the eye. "You tell us, Mr. Daniels. Have you done anything wrong?"

"No! I swear! I could never hurt Kristy!" he said vehemently.

"And why is that?" Vince purred.

"Because I..." Gregory started, then bit his bottom lip.

"Because you what, Gregory?"

"Because I loved her, okay?" he yelled. His eyes went wide as he realized what he had just proclaimed. Coming out from behind the desk, he ran from the office, tears streaming down his face.

Vince and Audrey looked at one another. "Well, okay then," Vince started, stuffing his notebook in his pocket again. "He certainly makes my short list of suspects."

Audrey thoughtfully peered out the glass door, watching Gregory vomit into a nearby flowerbed. "For Kristy, maybe. But Monica? What's the motive, Vince?"

Following her gaze, he conceded. "Good point. Let's go check out her apartment. Who knows, maybe we'll get lucky and find something."

Returning to the path outside the office, Vince turned to face her, a mischievous look twinkling in his eyes. "Kristy's apartment was number one sixty-nine."

"Please tell me you aren't about to make a sex joke with that," Audrey scolded.

"Damn, you beat me!" he chuckled.

Audrey rolled her eyes. "Focus, Vince. We need to go check her apartment for clues."

As they were talking, a young man in his early twenties approached, his dark hair falling rakishly in his gray eyes. "You here about Monica?" he asked.

"Actually, no," Audrey answered.

"Another tenant was found murdered this morning," Vince told him, watching his face closely.

"Wha—who, man?"

"Kristy Hillman."

"Kristy? Damn... that blows," the young man whistled. Catching Vince's curious gaze, he clarified. "She was a pistol, man."

"Sounds like you knew her well," Vince stated.

"Sure, I banged her once or twice," he replied.

"Seriously?" Audrey asked, incredulous.

"What?" he said, startled by her outburst. "Kristy liked sex," he shrugged.

"Un-huh. What's your name?" she muttered, pulling out her notebook.

"Edward Wright..." he said, suddenly wary.

"And Edward, when did you last see Kristy Hillman?"

"Um... not since last Wednesday, I guess," Edward answered after a moment's contemplation. "I drove up to Portland Friday for a concert. Ended up with a wicked hangover, so just got back now."

"Anyone who can verify that?" Vince asked.

"You want the name of the chick I partied with all weekend? I think she does discounts for law personnel."

"Oh, for the love of..." Audrey breathed. Turning to her partner, she was practically steaming. "Vince, he's clueless."

"Hey!" Edward protested.

"Zip it, horndog," she snapped. "Let's just go check out the apartment," she said, flipping her book closed.

As she started to walk away, Edward rubbed the back of his neck nervously. "Um..."

"What?" Audrey asked, turning to regard him with flashing eyes.

"Just thought you might want to talk to Barbara Snyder."

"Who's Barbara Snyder?" Vince asked.

Turning to face Vince, Edward became animated again. "She lives in apartment one seventy-five. That old bat sees everything. Once, she ratted on me for—"

"Do you really want to finish that sentence with two cops here?" Audrey interrupted.

"Good point," Edward said. "Have a nice day, officers!" he waved, running off.

"That kid is an idiot," Audrey said, shaking her head. Vince laughed beside her as she turned toward the row of apartments. "Reminds me of you sometimes..."

Vince's laughter cut off as he stared after her in annoyance. She was like the sister he'd never had, and it showed in their conversations.

"You coming?" she called over her shoulder.

He dusted himself off and began following her. Under his breath he muttered, "Yeah, I'm coming, you ballbuster."

A few minutes later they were being shown into Barbara Snyder's apartment, complete with their spring green walls. The elderly woman was the very definition of eclectic, Audrey thought as they followed her to the couch.

"Thanks for agreeing to speak with us, Mrs. Snyder," she said, hoping to get off on the right foot.

"Oh, don't mention it, dear! How could I refuse a handsome young man like your partner?" Barbara crooned.

How indeed? Audrey thought in disgust. There was an age gap of at least thirty years between the two. *Ick.*

"Would you like to sit down?" the older woman offered.

"That would be nice, ma'am," Vince answered.

They all took places on the furniture around them, Barbara in a large easy chair, and the detectives perched on her cream couch. When they had all settled, Barbara looked at them expectantly. "Now, what can I help you with today?"

"Mrs. Snyder—" Vince began.

"Barbara is fine, sugar," she corrected.

"Okay... Barbara..." he coughed.

Are all women just drawn to him? Must be the Italian side, Audrey mused. To his credit, Vince appeared more than a little uncomfortable with the attention from the grandmother-esque woman before him.

"How well did you know your neighbor, Kristy Hillman?" he asked.

"The walls are quite thin here, so well enough," Barbara answered. "But why are we talking about Kristy? I thought it was Monica you would be asking about."

"Barbara, Kristy was found murdered this morning," Audrey clarified.

Barbara's wrinkled hand flew to her heart. "Well, bless my soul," she breathed. "That poor little harlot finally met the wrong man."

"Care to elaborate?" Vince asked, clearly upset by the way she spoke.

"Oh my, now handsome, don't you know it's not right to talk ill of the dead?" Barbara scolded.

"Seeing as how you just called her a harlot, I think

we can continue," Audrey snapped.

"Well, I never!"

"Really, Barbara, we could use your help," Vince said soothingly, laying a hand on her knee.

"Fine," she huffed, her taupe eyes looking buggy behind her thick frames. "Kristy Hillman is—was—a bit of a wild woman. I can't tell you the number of men I've seen going up to her place. And not always just men, either. I seem to recall one time she and Monica spent the night together."

"You serious?" Vince asked in shock.

"Unfortunately, that's quite true," Audrey answered, hoping to keep Vince from drooling too much. "They got plastered at book club one night."

"Holy—"

"Watch your tongue in my house, young man," Barbara admonished.

"Yes, of course," he replied. "I was just so surprised..."

"Sure, you were," Audrey grumbled.

"Will you shut up, Stevens?" he whispered back.

"What are you two muttering about? It's hard to hear you," Barbara said, crossing her arms over her red apron.

Motioning for her to continue, Audrey offered a small smile. "Nothing ma'am. You were saying?"

"Well, Kristy would often have others stay over, and then there were times she would disappear for the entire weekend. She would usually come back with those disgusting love bites all over."

"What about this past weekend?" Audrey interjected.

"I was surprised when she came home right after her book club Friday," Barbara admitted.

"Is that unusual?" Vince asked.

"A bit, yes."

"Did you notice anything else about that night? Or even over the weekend?" Audrey pondered.

"Well, I assumed she had another hot date Friday. Maybe an hour after she came home, I heard her door slam. I saw her walk to her car, and she was all dressed up with a weekend bag."

"Was there anyone with her?"

"No, sorry, but I only saw her."

Audrey glanced up from her notebook. "Did you see her come back?"

"I didn't," Barbara confessed, "but her car was back yesterday morning when I woke up."

Vince shared an uneasy look with Audrey. "That's odd," he stated softly.

"I didn't see or hear her after Friday night. I assumed maybe she ended up sick and staying home," Barbara continued.

"Do you know anything about Kristy and Mr. Daniels?" Audrey asked.

"Gregory?" she squawked. "Oh, bless his awkward little soul. I know Gregory thought she was pretty, and don't get me wrong, she was. But Gregory is a bit backward where relationships are concerned.

"What do you mean?" asked Vince.

"You know, he's in his thirties, and I don't think he's ever been on a date," Barbara confided. "Wouldn't surprise me one bit if that poor thing dies a virgin."

"Would he ever hurt Kristy?"

Barbara looked at Audrey horrified. "Hurt anyone? Oh, honey, Gregory can't hurt a fly. He hates calling the pest company to deal with mice. He says they're God's creatures and deserve to live. Gregory may have been interested in Kristy, but he would never have done anything to her."

Silence descended upon them, the detectives feeling at another dead end. "Can you think of anything else?" Audrey asked.

Barbara thought in earnest for a moment and shook her head. "At the moment, no."

They all rose from their seats, Vince flashing her a smile. "Thanks so much for your help, Barbara."

"Oh, any time, detective," she blushed.

"If you think of anything else, please give us a call," Audrey interrupted, handing her a business card.

"Absolutely. Good luck, detectives!"

Audrey and Vince headed up the stairs to Kristy's apartment. Using the key they both knew Kristy kept in the planter by her front door, they let themselves into the room decorated in tones of purple and black, and looked around as their eyes adjusted. "Okay... so what are we looking for, exactly?"

"Anything that looks out of place, Vince. Signs of a struggle, or that she left against her will."

"Drey, everything looks exactly like it did when I was here before," he said, taking in the room once more.

"That was six months ago, and I know you've had sex since then," Audrey countered.

"And your point is?" he asked, annoyed.

"My point, Vincent, is how can you be sure?"

"Because I'm a detective and have an amazing memory, remember?" he said with a wink.

Rolling her eyes, Audrey faced him. "Okay, Casanova, walk me through your thought process."

Gesturing as he went, Vince explained. "Her bed is neatly made, and the desk is tidy. The place looks just as clean as she always kept it. There aren't any drawers left open or clothes hanging out, which suggests she didn't pack in a hurry to leave."

"Vince, did you see her car downstairs?" Audrey asked suddenly.

"No, why?"

"Because Snyder said she saw it back there yesterday morning."

"But she didn't see or hear Kristy yesterday..."

Heading for the door, Audrey told him, "I'm going to go check the parking lot really quick. Maybe we missed something."

"Okay, I'll keep looking in here," he answered, turning his gaze back to the bed.

————◆•◆————

Mere moments later, Audrey came back in through the door. Vince looked up from the notebook on the desk as she entered. "Find anything in here?"

"Nothing. You?"

"Didn't have to," she answered.

"Huh?"

"Lawson just called," Audrey explained. "Apparently some hikers found Kristy's car about thirty miles away."

"What the hell? That makes absolutely no sense, Drey."

"You're telling me," she said exhausted. "The car is being towed to the lab now."

Shrugging, Vince looked at her expectantly. "So now what?"

"You ready to go back to the precinct?"

"Guess so, Drey. I'll drive."

————◆•◆————

The sun was setting as they sat at their desks, folders littering the tops. With tired eyes, Vince looked over at his partner. "Is it just me, or are we going to be here awhile?"

Sighing, Audrey let the folder she'd been holding fall onto her desk. "Oh, definitely will—" Her face snapped up as she saw the time on her phone. "Crap!"

"What?" Vince asked, concerned.

"I was supposed to be going to dinner with Declan tonight," she moaned.

Relief that it wasn't something more serious, Vince set his own folder down gently. "I'm sure I can cover for you if you want to go."

"No, it's okay. He knew who he was marrying."

"A workaholic?" Vince joked.

"Hush," she scolded with a giggle. "Guess I better call him and break the news."

"I'll be quiet."

"That'll be a first," Audrey teased. Vince stuck his tongue out at her as she hit the button to call her husband.

"Hey, baby girl, you on your way home?" Declan asked cheerily.

"About that..."

"Audrey, what's up?"

"So, that homicide this morning..." she trailed.

"Yeah? Has it been bad?" he asked.

She sighed. "You have no idea, Dec. It was Kristy."

"Kristy?" she heard him breathe. "Oh my God, Audrey. I'm so sorry, honey. Are you all right?"

"Honestly, I'm not sure how I am at the moment," she told him. "I'm just trying to get through today."

"Well, come on home and we can have some dinner. I'll rub your back and take your mind off work," Declan invited.

"As amazing as that sounds..." she started, sharing a worried look with Vince.

"Audrey, you need to take a break. Especially now that you've lost two friends so close together."

"I know. And I really appreciate you looking out for me. There's a good possibility, though, that this is connected."

"Audrey," he said, attempting to control his voice over the phone, "are you trying to say Monica and Kristy's deaths are related? Like we may have a serial killer in Ashland, related?"

"Yeah, baby, I am."

Vince looked up in shock as Declan's next words echoed across the desk. "Audrey Verona Stevens, get your ass home now!"

Audrey's face went from tired to hard in an instant at his words. Her knuckles turned a bit white as she gripped the phone before answering him. "What did you just tell me?"

"You heard me the first time. I want you where I know you're safe."

Vince shifted uncomfortably in his seat, wishing he could be somewhere, anywhere else in that moment. "Declan, did you forget what my job is? I will be home after I help go through the evidence. I was simply calling as a courtesy."

"Audrey—" Declan warned, but she cut him off with an icy tone.

"I will talk to you later!"

She punched the button to end the call, and probably would have thrown the phone onto the table if it wouldn't have broken.

"Are you all right?"

Refusing to meet his eyes, she started reorganizing the folders on her desk. "Let's just get back to work, Cortenza."

"Audrey, really…" he protested.

"I said, let's get back to work," she snapped. "I'm not taking marital advice from you tonight."

"Okay, okay… you win! I surrender, warrior queen," Vince told her.

Looking back at the crime scene photos, Audrey held back a look of satisfaction. *Damn right, I win…*

CHAPTER THREE

Wednesday morning dawned bright and clear in Ashland. At the early hour of 7:26 a.m., Samantha Ross—Sam, to everyone else—walked down the hall at the office of the *Ashland Daily Tidings* newspaper in search of her top reporter. Her heels clicked on the tiled floor, echoing softly in the still quiet building. Unfazed, she saw the light filtering under the door at the end of the hall, having known before she left her own office that Ellsie Lewis would already be at work.

Rapping lightly on the door before entering, she found the young red-headed woman typing furiously on her laptop. Ellsie's eyes flicked from her screen to her boss's face as Sam entered the room, her fingers stilling instantly.

"Ellsie, you got a minute?"

"For you?" she teased. "Anytime. What's up, Sam?"

Sam tossed her platinum blonde hair over her shoulder and rubbed the back of her bronzed neck. "We've got a real hot story coming in, and I want you to cover it."

"What kind of story?"

"It's looking like we may have a serial killer in our midst..." Sam said.

"You're kidding!" Ellsie exclaimed, her green eyes going wide. "That's... scary, Sam."

Sam nodded in agreement. "Yeah, it's bad. Chief Mitchel asked for my best reporter, and we both know that's you, honey. And speaking of the best, Vincent Cortenza and Audrey Stevens are assigned to the case."

Ellsie flushed at the mention of the attractive Detective Cortenza's name. The man was drop-dead gorgeous, and everyone in Ashland knew it. Ellsie struggled to compose herself, fiddling with the chain of her looped necklace before meeting Sam's dark eyes once more.

"Sounds good, Sam. I'll contact them this afternoon and get right on the story."

"I know you'll do a great job, girl," Sam assured her, turning to the door. She hadn't made it more than a few steps before she paused and glanced back at the reporter still seated at her desk. "Ellsie?"

"Yeah?"

"Do me a favor and be careful on this one. I would hate to lose one of my bright stars," Sam said quietly.

Ellsie saw the fear lodged deep in her boss's eyes and knew something must be terribly amiss for Sam to be worried enough to voice a concern. She managed a small smile and nodded. "I'll do my best."

Her confidence returning, Sam shot Ellsie a dazzling smile and departed, leaving Ellsie to stare absently at her laptop. Neither could imagine the daunting task this story would prove to be, and neither was prepared for twisted turn of events steaming toward them.

———•———

Across town in a cheery florist shop, Chloe Harper was hard at work replacing tulips and roses in the various jars around the workbench. Her assistant, Liliana, was rummaging in the back room, flowers strewn across her table as she worked. As Chloe retuned to the counter, Liliana poked her head into the shop.

"Hey, Chloe?"

"Yes?"

"Have we gotten the lily shipment in yet?" she asked, stepping fully into the room.

"It's due in this afternoon," Chloe told her, lightly stretching.

"Dang!"

"Trouble?"

"I just needed half a dozen to finish this arrangement I'm working on," Liliana grumbled.

Chloe giggled, her light brown hair coming loose from its braid to wisp around her face. She had opened this shop two years before, and Liliana had been her assistant for the past ten months. And while she loved the other girl and her dedication to excellent floral care, Chloe was always shaking her head at Lil's theatrics.

"Be patient, Lils," she answered as the chime over the door chirped to life. Chloe turned to face their new customer and felt Liliana shrink into the doorway behind her. "Hey, Declan."

"I'll just get back to work..." Liliana trailed before making a hasty retreat into the workroom.

Declan stared after her, his ice-blue eyes looking inquisitively under furrowed brows. "What's her problem?" he queried.

"Don't pay any attention to her," Chloe reassured him. "She's a scaredy-cat. So, what brings you by my shop today?"

"Well..." he started, rubbing the back of his neck sheepishly.

Chloe chuckled and shook her head at her best friend's husband. "What did you do, Declan?"

"I may have yelled at Audrey last night," he whispered.

"I'm sorry, what was that? It sounded like something extremely foolish just came out of your mouth."

"That's about right, Chloe," Declan replied. "I yelled at Audrey last night over the phone."

Chloe looked incredulously at him. Although she knew he was a laid-back person, she also had seen he had a fairly mild temper. Audrey on the other hand... when you pissed her off, you better be prepared for all hell to break loose.

"Do you have a death wish, Declan?"

He laughed softly at her vehement exclamation. Tossing her a small smile, he shrugged. "You'd think, huh? She started working a new case yesterday and then ditched our date night to work. I was snarky in turn."

"Declan," Chloe gently reprimanded, "you do

realize her job is to work cases, right? And we both know she loves her job."

"Yeah, yeah," he grumbled. "It doesn't mean I have to like taking a back seat all the time. I have needs, too, Chloe."

Putting her hands up in surrender, Chloe's voice softened. "Never said you didn't."

Declan sighed deeply and ran a hand through his tousled dark hair. His eyes slid up and down her body appreciatively, causing the blood to rush to her cheeks. He leaned against the counter, his eyes lingering on her peach lips.

"By the way, you're glowing, Chloe," he told her, his voice deep and husky.

Her blush deepened at his words.

"I mean it, Chloe. There is something so beautiful about a woman with child."

Unconsciously, her hand stroked the slight swell of her child under her blue top. Only in the past few weeks had she began wearing maternity clothes, her pregnancy still in the early weeks. Audrey and Declan had already agreed to be her child's godparents, and they would announce this decision at the gender reveal party to be held in a month.

"Declan, you're making me blush," she said, biting on her lower lip.

"I'm just being honest," he replied with a wink.

Straightening her top, she attempted to collect herself. "Well, thank you. It's nice to hear that every so often." *Especially since David has been more concerned over the financial impact of the baby than the baby itself. That's what I get for marrying a banker.*

"I'm guessing you're here to get something as an apology for Audrey?"

"Right, Audrey. Yes," he stuttered. "What would you recommend, sweetness?"

"You can't go wrong with roses, Declan. Besides, I'm pretty sure those are her favorite flowers, right?" she asked as she gestured to the vases nearby.

"You would be right about that, Chloe. The darker the red, the better."

Chloe pulled out her order pad and began making notes. "Okay, I can do that. Are we doing a dozen... ?" she trailed, looking up expectantly.

"Make it six dozen," he said, rubbing the back of his neck again.

"You must have really screwed up, Declan," Chloe told him as she wrote up his bill.

"You have no idea. Can you send those to the house, please?"

"You got it. Give me a couple hours and I'll drop them off."

"Sounds good, little momma. And I'm going to have another order for you later."

"Aren't you in a giving mood today?" she teased.

"See you later, Chlo," Declan responded, heading out the door with a wave.

Chloe smiled and shook her head and turned to start prepping his order. She passed Liliana coming from the rear room and took over the table in the back to assemble the roses. Meanwhile, a customer Chloe hadn't realized was still in the shop quietly slipped outside without making a purchase. Pulling her phone from her purse, Shannon Mitchel began looking through her contacts.

Interesting, very interesting, she thought. *I wonder if Audrey knows what her husband's up to?* Shannon waited impatiently as her phone rang and nervously greeted her friend when she picked up the call.

"Hey, Audrey. You got a second?"

"Sure, Shannon. What's up?" Audrey's voice asked, tiredness seeping through her tone.

"Just wanted to see if you had a couple minutes to get coffee later. I know you started a new case yesterday, but—"

"Did Shawn give you any details?" Audrey interrupted.

"About Monica and Kristy, you mean? Yeah, he mentioned you guys linked their deaths. It's insanity," Shannon said sadly.

"It is. Sucks that our book club has lost two members now... and we've lost some great friends," Audrey admitted. "I'm actually getting ready to take a quick break now. Would you want to meet in ten?"

"That sounds like a plan. I'll see you at the corner café soon."

Shannon ended the call and slowly replaced her phone in her purse. Dread seemed to be gripping her heart as she looked down the street where the café was located. She hated the fact she would be the one potentially to break her friend's heart by telling her about Declan.

If it were the other way around, I would want her to tell me about Shawn, she reasoned. *She deserves to know he was flirting with another woman... especially since it was her best friend! Who is very much married herself and pregnant, for goodness sake!*

"Suck it up, Shannon," she murmured to herself. "Get your ass down the street and let her know what just happened." *And pray she doesn't decide to shoot the messenger...*

⸺ ◆ ⸺

Fifteen minutes later, Shannon sat nervously in a table near the back of the small café. Two cups of coffee rested on the table before her, steaming rising from the small holes in the lids. Shannon's eyes darted around the café every few seconds, the anticipation almost more than she could bear.

Finally, Audrey walked through the door, and Shannon waved her over. "Audrey!"

Audrey's blonde head swiveled to find her friend and made her way across the room to join her. Shannon stood as Audrey approached, stepping around the chairs to embrace the other woman. "Hey, Shannon."

Together they sat at the table by the windows, taking sips of their coffees as they looked out at the town passing by. Shannon warmed her hands on her cup and eyed Audrey before speaking. "Thanks for meeting me," she said quietly.

"Not a problem. I was desperately needing some caffeine after the night I had working," Audrey replied. "So, thanks for this, Shan."

"Have you heard from Bridget yet?" Shannon asked.

"Thankfully, no," Audrey said, exhausted. "You and I both know she's going to hit the roof when she finds out about Kristy."

Shannon dropped her head into her hands in frustration, thinking of their book club president. "Yeah, and not for the right reasons," she agreed. "You and I both know Bridget is a bit eccentric."

Audrey chuckled. "Book club should be interesting on Friday."

Shannon paused to consider her words. Two of their members had died suspiciously in less than two weeks. It was sure to be upsetting for most of the members of the club. Bridget Middleton, however... who could say how she would truly react?

"Do you think we'll still have it this week?"

"I kinda doubt Bridget will cancel; you know what she's like," Audrey answered. "Although, at this rate, I may not make it."

"Case not going well?"

Audrey sighed heavily and looking down at the table. She studied the grooves in the wood for a moment before speaking. She knew Shannon would keep any information she shared to herself, her relationship with Shawn practically ensured this.

"So far, it seems like we don't have any evidence. I'm actually worried we'll have to wait for another victim to learn anything," she confessed.

Sucking in a sharp breath, Shannon looked at the weary expression on Audrey's face. "You don't really believe that, do you?"

"Sadly, yes. Shannon, I'm afraid we won't make the connections before this killer strikes again. Whoever it is, they're smart. Vince and I worked almost all night, too."

"Speaking of work..." Shannon trailed.

"Shannon, you know I'm not at liberty to divulge any details. I've already told you more than I would tell most people just because of your connection with Shawn," Audrey warned.

"Oh... no, not about the case," Shannon said, rubbing her neck.

Audrey looked skeptically at Shannon. "What, then?"

"What does Declan think about the case?"

Rolling her eyes sarcastically, Audrey looked over the top of her coffee cup. "Did he call you to complain that I missed our date last night?"

"No... but..."

"He knew what I did when we got married."

"Yeah, but when was the last time you two had a date?"

Crossing her arms over her chest, Audrey's eyes glossed over in anger as she stared at Shannon. A frown etched itself in her face, and she glared at her friend. *Declan, and my relationship with him, is an off-limits subject,* she thought to herself.

"Shannon... mind your own business," she said before standing up. "Look, thanks for the coffee, but I gotta go."

Audrey turned away and walked a couple steps before Shannon called after her. "Audrey, wait."

"What?" she snapped. "I'm kinda busy."

"Yeah, but I think you might want to call Declan," Shannon urged.

"He's going to have to deal with my job right now. I don't have time for dates, or book clubs, or..." she threw her hands up in exasperation. She tried to walk away again, but Shannon grabbed her arm.

"Audrey!"

"Sheesh... what?" she exploded.

"I saw Declan flirting with Chloe," Shannon blurted.

Audrey reeled in shock, her blue eyes wide in disbelief. "I'm sorry... what?" she sputtered.

"At the florist shop just an hour ago. Declan was flirting with Chloe," Shannon haltingly explained.

"You've got to be kidding me," Audrey said angrily. "I don't have time for jokes today!"

"I wish I were joking, Audrey," Shannon said sadly. "I think he's tired of taking a back seat to your job."

———•———

Thirty minutes after her confrontation with Shannon, Audrey stormed into her black and white kitchen, the glass reflecting the sunlight and her husband arranging a large vase of dark red roses. His ice-blue eyes reflecting the light streaming in the windows as well as he saw her enter.

"Declan Howell Stevens!" she yelled.

The look in his eyes went from happiness to shock at her tone.

With toxicity dripping in her voice, Audrey screamed, "Anything you want to confess?"

———•———

Back at the precinct, Vince and Sarah were flipping through files when she happened to notice the time. Looking over at the handsome detective, she wondered if she should even be questioning him, but felt she needed to voice a concern.

"Hey, Cortenza?"

"Yeah?" he said, not looking up from the file he was reading.

"Shouldn't Detective Stevens be back by now?" Vince finally set down his file and looked at the rookie across from him. Sarah rubbed her arm, nervous to be under his gaze. "It's just... she left for coffee more than an hour ago..."

"Yes... yes, she did," Vince agreed thoughtfully. "Interesting."

"You don't think it became too much for her, do you?"

"Huh? Oh... no ," Vince replied, picking up the file once more. "She was going to meet Shannon Mitchel."

"The chief's wife?" Sarah asked, incredulous.

"Yeah, they're friends," Vince said with a shrug. "They also are both part of the same book club as our vics. Chances are high they're talking about that. Shannon knows what she can and can't ask, but they could be preparing themselves for Friday."

"What's Friday?"

"It's when their book club meets."

Sarah looked at him and nodded. "Oh, right. Speaking of their book club, has anyone interviewed them?"

Vince pointed at the notepad on the desk. "It's on the to-do list. Up until you connected the cases, Monica's death was ruled differently. 'Accidental drowning under suspicious circumstances.'"

"I'm not very familiar with any of the case details for her," Sarah admitted.

Vince looked at her with a flirtatious twinkle in his dark brown eyes. "Want me to get you caught up, Lawson?"

Hell to the yes, Sarah thought excitedly. She blushed to the roots of her hair and prayed Vince's sharp eyes didn't notice. She saw his eyebrows raise in question. "That would be very helpful."

He winked. "That's me, *Bellissima*. Helpful."

"*Bellissima*?"

"Not familiar with Italian?" he said with a smile. "I may have to rectify that situation later. So, last Monday we found Monica's body at the base of Klamath Falls."

"At the base?"

"Yeah, some hikers had found her washed up on the shore..."

— ◆ —

Monday, September 30, 2019
11:15 a.m.

Standing at the top of the cliff, Vince and Audrey searched the base below. Vince removed his sunglasses and scanned the edge of the woods surrounding the pool formed beneath the waterfall. His brown eyes glinted with sunlight as he faced his partner.

"Do you see them?"

"There they are," she told him, pointing to the far side of the pool. "All the way at the bottom."

"Hope you wore your hiking boots, Drey," he snickered.

Audrey faced him and smirked. "You and I both know I'll beat you down there, Vince. Don't try to pretend you're more outdoorsy than me."

A few minutes later, Audrey stepped off the path at the bottom and brushed her long blonde hair from her face. Behind her, Vince puffed as he followed her. Audrey struggled to keep the grin off her face.

"You going to make it, Cortenza? You're breathing awfully hard," she laughed.

"Bite me, Stevens," he answered, flipping her off in the process.

One of the paramedics turned their way, having heard their banter. She waved them over to where she and Henry Winters stood. "Hey, Audrey. Vince."

"Cathy," Audrey intoned. "What do we have?"

"Some hikers found her this morning. It looks like she may have fallen from the cliff and drowned. There's a pretty wicked cut on her forehead," Cathy announced.

"Got an ID yet?" Vincent asked.

Henry piped up, "We didn't need one. We all recognized her despite the elements putting her through hell." He coughed, clearly uncomfortable in continuing. "It's Monica Simpson."

"Monica?" Audrey gasped, one hand covering her mouth in horror. "Oh God, no!"

Vince pulled her into his arms to keep her from lunging at the body behind Cathy and Henry, his own face contorted with a mixture of disbelief and grief. "Damn!" he exclaimed. "I never would have expected this. She was always so careful when she hiked."

Henry shrugged. "Yeah, but we had that freak storm kick up a couple days ago, remember? She may have been caught off guard."

Audrey looked up from Vince's chest, her eyes

glistening with tears. "A couple days? How long do you think she's been dead?"

"Blake thought it looked like three to four days, Audrey," Cathy replied.

Audrey's eyes went wider still. Vince felt her legs begin to go out from under her and did his best to keep her on her feet. "But... but... that's not possible!" she stammered. "She was just sick last week!"

Vince turned to her in question, his arm still supporting her. "Audrey?"

"She missed book club last week, but she had called Bridget. Said she ended up with the flu," she answered. "Why would she be here?"

He looked thoughtfully at her and then back at Monica's body. "She doesn't live too far away. Maybe she went out to get some meds and got lost."

"Or was starting to feel better and tried to do too much at once," Henry offered.

"Or she could have faked being sick to get out of something else..." Cathy suggested.

"I... I don't know what to make of this right now," Audrey murmured.

All three of them looked with compassion at the level-headed detective. Audrey was not one for emotional outbursts, so they knew this was taking a toll on her. Both Cathy and Henry shifted nervously and waited for Vincent to break the ice.

"Why don't you head back up to the car, Drey. I'll stay here to make sure things get wrapped up, okay?"

Audrey sighed and nodded as tears continued to fill

her eyes. "Thanks, Vince." Slowly she made her way back up the path toward their car.

Vince turned back to Cathy and Henry as she faded around the corner of the trees, doing his best to mask his own emotions.

"Is she going to be okay?" Cathy asked timidly.

Vince glanced back at his partner before answering. "God, I hope so..."

Sarah looked at him in awe as he finished outlining the Monday prior. "I can't even imagine what must be going through her head..." she sighed.

"Going through whose head?" came a feminine voice behind them.

They turned to find Audrey standing a few feet away, her hands resting lightly on her hips. Sarah gasped at having her so close and Vince raised an eyebrow in question.

"Detective Stevens! You're back!" Sarah said, stating the obvious.

"Drey, everything all right?"

"Oh yes, just a misunderstanding that needed to be dealt with, Vince," Audrey assured him. Unfortunately, it merely piqued his interest more.

"What misunderstanding?"

Audrey ignored him and moved closer to the desk, reaching for the nearest file. Vince grabbed her wrist and forced her to face him. An unwavering look crossed his face, and he waited impatiently for her to explain.

"Someone was telling Shannon and me that Declan was flirting with another woman," she stated with a slight shrug.

"*Mi stai prendendo in giro!*" Vince yelped.

"Nope, not kidding you. Sadly, someone was convinced he was flirting."

Sarah looked with amazement between them. "You understood him?"

Audrey's gaze flicked to the other woman before she giggled. "You work with this *perdente* long enough, you pick up some things."

He raised his hands in defense. "I am not a loser, Drey."

Audrey rolled her eyes in response and smirked. "So, was your husband guilty?" he asked.

She turned away from them to look at the files spread across the desk, answering as she flipped through one. "No, but I can see why they thought he was."

Vince searched her with yet another question in his dark eyes. "Who accused him?"

"I'd rather not say, Vince. What were you working on when I came in?"

"Vince—I mean, Detective Cortenza—was getting me caught up on the Simpson case," Lawson offered.

"We have photos of both scenes if you want to look," Vince told her.

"Sure, let's head to the layout room and get started," Audrey responded.

———•———

Friday, October 11, 2019
3:12 p.m.

Standing in the layout room, Shawn, Vince, Audrey, and Sarah looked at the photos pinned to the bulletin board, evidence boxes littering the table behind them. Shawn rubbed his jaw thoughtfully as he looked at the gruesome images.

"So, tell me where we're at now," he said quietly.

"Not much farther than we were two days ago, Shawn," Audrey admitted in defeat.

Dark circles rimmed her eyes, and her blonde hair was slightly disheveled from the long hours. Vince didn't look much better. Stubble covered his chiseled jaw more than usual, and his clothes were wrinkled. Sarah and Shawn were the only ones who seemed to have gotten much sleep in the past forty-eight hours.

"Sadly, she's right," Vince confirmed, his hand running down his face in exhaustion.

Nervously, Sarah chimed in, gesturing to the board as she spoke. "As you can see, Chief, the only thing we've connected are the dice."

"That's the only thing that's the same in both cases?" When all three nodded, Shawn's face hardened. "Damn!"

"At this rate, I'm worried we won't ever catch this psycho," confessed Audrey.

"I can run the evidence again with Denise..." Sarah started.

"That's a great start, Sarah, but we've got to think long term," Vince interrupted.

Sarah looked at him questioningly, catching Audrey's eyes in the process. Audrey smiled gently at her, knowing the rookie was getting thrown in the deep end of the pool with her very first case.

"He means we need to try to profile this guy to prevent further deaths, Lawson," she explained.

"Audrey, you're the best at that," Shawn stated. "What are you thinking?"

They all paused to consider what they knew. Audrey turned away to look at the crime scene photos briefly, then turned back to the fellow officers. "Whoever this is, he's highly intelligent, probably a loner who lives outside of city limits..."

"That would make sense, I suppose," Shawn said. "Kristy's murder was clearly messy, but judging by the crime scene, she was murdered elsewhere before the killer dumped her body in the woods."

"So, whoever this guy is, he probably has a place to work where they can be undiscovered," Audrey concluded.

"Do you know how many people live outside city limits, Drey?" Vince asked in frustration.

"Too many, Vince. Too many," she confirmed.

They stood in silence momentarily before Shawn's phone began ringing. He looked at it, perplexed, answering with concern in his voice. "Shannon?"

Vince turned to face their boss as the ladies shifted uneasily.

"Babe... slow down, I can't understand you," Shawn continued.

Through the phone they could all hear the garbled panic in Shannon's voice as she spoke. "Shannon, you're breaking up, honey. Shannon? Shannon? Shannon!" Shawn exclaimed.

He stared at his phone with wide eyes, fear crippling him. Vince laid a hand on his shoulder, while Audrey's eyes filled with tears and Sarah clasped a hand over her mouth.

"I... I have to try to find her," Shawn stammered.

As he fled the room, Audrey's phone chirped. Glancing at the caller ID, she answered tiredly. "Hey, David. What's going on? Slow down, David," she said, snapping her fingers to get Vince's attention. "What do you mean you think Chloe is missing?"

Vince's eyes widened in surprise, and Sarah collapsed in a nearby chair. Audrey herself gripped the edge of the table for support, her legs nearly giving out beneath her.

"David, I'm going to put you on speaker. Hang on a second."

"Chloe was supposed to go out for lunch," David Harper explained over the line. "Her assistant, Liliana, just called me to say she never came back! Audrey, I know something is going on in this town, so tell me where my wife is!"

"David, I have no idea. I will do everything in my

power to find her though. You know that, right?" Audrey reassured him.

"Chloe loves you like a sister, but I need answers now, not later."

"David, Audrey and I will get right on her disappearance," Vince chimed.

"See that you do," David answered angrily before hanging up.

"Oh my God," Sarah breathed.

"Yeah. Two women disappearing in the span of a few hours. What kind of game is this psycho playing?" Vince growled.

Looking up from the table, tears running down her face as she looked at the crime scene photos of two of her other friends, Audrey said resignedly, "It sounds like a little game called murder, Vince."

CHAPTER FOUR

Saturday, October 12, 2019
9:38 a.m.

"Oh my God, have you heard?"
  "I know! It's so crazy!"
  "Who would have guessed, right?"
  "It's downright scary!"
  "What do you think the cops are doing about it?"
  "I heard hottie Cortenza was on the case!"
  "Don't forget about Audrey Stevens, too."
  "The whole situation makes you think, doesn't it?"
  "Yeah... who'll be next... ?"

— • —

Seated at her desk, Ellsie Lewis pressed disconnect on her phone, aggravation pounding through her veins. It had only been a day since the latest two women disappeared, and already the rumors were spreading like wildfires. In small towns, mystery and scandals had a tendency to overshadow everything. When the rumor mills kicked into high gear, they made her job twice as difficult as she had to balance keeping the general public informed and not causing mass chaos and panic.

She groaned as she starred at the cell phone on her desk, her laptop screen glowing behind her. "Geez, this rumor mill is a mess," she muttered, running a hand through her red hair. "I better give Audrey a heads-up. This is going to piss her off royally."

Sighing, Ellsie picked up her phone and dialed the detective. Audrey was the easier one to talk to, despite her temper, namely because Ellsie found herself tongue-tied every time she attempted to speak with Vince. She didn't have long to wait as Audrey answered promptly.

"Detective Stevens."

"Hi, detective, this is Ellsie Lewis," she began.

"I don't have time for an interview at the moment, Ellsie," Audrey replied.

"I realize you're quite busy, but I thought you might want a warning that the rumor mill is buzzing with suspicions and misinformation," Ellsie told her.

"Fan-freaking-tastic," Audrey exploded. "This is just what we needed." The sarcasm dripped heavily through the phone, and Ellsie felt herself shrinking further into her seat.

"If you want to give me a few facts to publish, I can attempt to quiet some of it for you."

Audrey sighed as she contemplated the reporter's idea. Giving the public a few facts could help quell the fear and potentially aid them in solving the cases. Too many facts could lead to a copycat killer, which was the last thing they needed at present.

"That's not a bad idea. Let me go grab Vince and

we'll give you an exclusive in a few hours, okay?"

"Sounds fair," Ellsie answered breathlessly. "I'll see you later."

Get a grip, Lewis...

"Hey, rookie, let's move," Audrey announced wearily, looking across the desk at Sarah. Sarah quickly set down the file she had been reading, her hazel eyes bright with curiosity.

"Detective?"

"That was Ellsie Lewis at the paper. Apparently, the rumor mill has decided to be extra involved in this case already, so we need to get Vince so we can get back to work," Audrey explained.

"Oh, okay. Where is he?" Sarah asked as she stood up and pushed in her chair.

"Where else?" Audrey said, rolling her eyes. "At the gym, where he's sure to be sans shirt and sweaty."

As they headed for the door, Sarah's mind was filled with images of Vince's chiseled abs on display. *I don't think I'd mind seeing that scene...*

Twelve minutes later, the pair entered the eerily quiet private gym Vince used. Scanning the room, they were surprised to find only Vince in the expansive space. He was rigorously pumping weights, his shirt gone, a white towel laid beside him. His biceps bulged as he lifted the curling bar loaded with weights in smooth reps.

Audrey cleared her throat, causing his head to snap in their direction. He stood up from the bench and picked up the towel after setting down the heavy bar, wiping beads of sweat from his brow. Perspiration continued to roll down his muscled chest, and he smirked at the heat painting Sarah's cheeks scarlet.

"See something you like, Lawson?"

"Uh..."

He chuckled as he came close, the sheen from the moisture on his body causing him almost to glow in the morning light. If Sarah were being honest, he looked like a sculpture of raw masculinity one might find in the museums in Italy or France. The man was downright, albeit sinfully, attractive.

"You seem to have the gym to yourself this morning, Vince," Audrey commented.

"Yeah, so I do," he replied, eyeing Sarah with a mischievous glint in his dark eyes. "Such a shame, actually. Perhaps you should join me for a quick workout, Sarah."

"Cortenza, are you capable of being anything less than a player for five minutes?" Audrey scolded.

"Oh, give me a break, Drey. I'm allowed to flirt with the rookie. Makes me feel alive in the midst of this nightmare," he answered as he wiped the sweat from his body.

"Fine, but feel alive after we've dealt with the latest crisis."

"Latest crisis?" Vince asked, pulling his t-shirt over his head.

"I just got a call from that reporter, Ellsie Lewis. Apparently, the rumor mill is in full swing and we need to help put an end to the panic gripping Ashland."

"Gotta love the gossipy harpies we have in this town, huh?" he said with a wink to Sarah.

"Go shower, please," Audrey said wrinkling her nose. "You stink."

"Guess that means you need a hug then!"

"Touch me and I'll pistol-whip you!" she shrieked, holding her hands out to repel him.

They all laughed, letting the mood dissipate into an uneasy silence that followed. Vince grabbed his bag and headed for the locker room while the ladies found a bench and checked emails on their phones.

Once in the car, Audrey brought Vince further up to speed. From the back seat, Sarah continued to look through their files on the cases they had been struggling with the past week. Vince glanced back at her, a question nagging at his brain.

"Hey, Lawson," he said, getting her attention. "What do we have on the trace reports?"

"Shockingly little, detective. In the Simpson case, there was nothing, thanks to her being in the water.

In the Hillman case, we have blood splatter that we are still waiting to hear back from the DNA lab for the results."

"Is that it?" Audrey asked.

"Yep," Sarah answered. "The lab said they were going to rush the results for us because of the circumstances."

"Do you have the book club interviews with you, Lawson?"

"Oops. No, I left them at the precinct."

"No problem, Stevens has a near-photographic memory," he told her. "Audrey, care to give me a recap?"

"Sure, Vincey."

"I thought I told you not to call me that again!"

Both ladies giggled at his indignation, and Audrey quickly began recounting the talk they'd had with her fellow book club members.

⸺•⸺

Thursday, October 10, 2019
10:16 a.m.

Bridget Middleton, Harriett Foster, Felicia Marcel, and Ilsa Ramirez had all come together to meet with Vince about the case concerning their two fallen members. Audrey had politely excused herself to allow for a less biased officer to conduct the interviews. However, having dated Felicia's twin sister, he wasn't completely impartial.

"So, ladies, thank you all for coming down here this morning," he began. "We just need to get some further information from you in regard to Monica and Kristy."

"Kristy was a tramp, end of story," Bridget stated, checking out her manicure.

"Bridget, that isn't kind," Harriett scolded. "She was a wild woman, but she had a good heart."

Bridget rolled her narrowed hazel eyes in the other woman's direction. Having been married to her husband, Elijah, for nearly ten years now, she considered anyone who had multiple partners as a tramp. The other women in the book club put up with her judgmental attitude most of the time, but this whole ordeal was taking its toll on them.

Felicia crossed her toffee arms over her slender chest and glared at Bridget in disdain. "Bridget, one would think you might learn to filter that mouth of yours in thirty-three years, but no. You persist in dripping toxic opinions every time you open those painted lines you call lips. So why don't you do us all a favor and keep quiet unless you happen to know something of true importance."

Vince found himself struggling to rein in the laughter threatening to bubble from his well-formed mouth as Felicia tore into the club president. The other ladies in attendance had a look that was a combination of horror and admiration as she forcefully knocked Bridget off her high horse. Bridget's eyes were practically glowing with hostility as she listened, her manicured nails gripping the edge of the table in anger.

"Vince, what would you like to know?" Felicia asked as she turned her back on the still-seething Bridget.

"What can you tell me about Monica's disappearance?"

"Up until you and Audrey connected her death to Kristy's, none of us thought much of it," Ilsa commented. "She had called me on Wednesday to say she had ended up with the flu after book club the week before and didn't think she'd make it Friday."

"That was the twenty-fifth, correct?"

"That's right," she answered, nodding her head.

"Did any of you ladies hear from her?"

They all paused to consider his question, and then slowly shook their heads.

"As you know, Monica was a member of the orchestra, so the other people who might know anything would be her fellow musicians," Felicia offered. "Wyatt and Hadley were her two closest friends, if I remember correctly."

"You happen to know their last names, Felicia?" Vince asked.

"Wyatt Smith and Hadley Janssen. Wyatt plays the violin and Hadley plays the clarinet, if that matters," she replied. "Monica played the flute, so she and Hadley spent the most time together. I think they may have even dated briefly."

"Okay, that's good to know," he said as he wrote. "Do you happen to know when their last practice would have been?"

"Sorry, no. From what I understood, it was a daily

practice during performance season, but since the orchestra was taking a month off while their theater underwent renovations, they all had plenty of down time," Felicia told him.

"What did Monica do for money in between performances?"

"She taught private lessons," Ilsa answered.

"Hmmm... do you know if she had any students currently?"

"Not a clue, detective."

Silence descended as Vince filled his notepad with information, waiting for someone else to speak out. Harriett squirmed in her seat, and timidly caught Vince's eyes. There was a faint flush burning on her chocolate cheeks, and she seemed woefully uncomfortable with what she was about to say.

"Kristy told me at book club that she had started flirting with a guy online," she began, Vince jotting notes as she spoke. "From what she gathered about him, he was married but in an open relationship, so his wife didn't mind him seeing other women..."

"Go on," Vince encouraged when she trailed off.

"The way she described everything, though, I don't think the wife knew about her. The husband wanted to keep Kristy a secret and not have to share her with his wife, I guess. She was all excited because she was finally going to meet him in person that night."

"That's why she was in such a rush to get out of book club that night?" Bridget raged. "Are you telling me she wanted to go engage in an extramarital affair *with a stranger? The nerve of some people!"*

Four pairs of eyes looked at her incredulously after her outburst. The tension between them all was so thick, it was palpable. Vince made a quick note on his pad, then returned to Harriett's story.

"Do you happen to know what site? The place she was planning to meet this guy, where he lived, anything?" Vince queried.

"I wish I knew more, detective," Harriett said quietly. "That's pretty much all I know."

"Do any of you other ladies have anything to add?"

They all shook their heads. "Okay, well if you think of anything in the coming days, please give us a call."

⸺ ♦ ⸺

The trio arrived back at the precinct to drop Sarah off, only to find the usually calm lobby in chaos. Officers were crowded in the tight space, the secretary clutching her heart in terror. All eyes were fixated on the door leading to Chief Mitchel's office. Over the sounds of murmurs rose the clamoring of furniture and desk objects being hurled against the walls.

"What the hell is going on?" Vince demanded.

"The chief— he's— he's—" the secretary stammered, tears clouding her vision.

Audrey and Vince pushed past the others and headed for the door. Sarah followed but kept her distance, remaining at the edge of the crowd of uniformed officers who looked on in disbelief. Audrey knocked lightly on the wooden door, but her knock went unanswered.

"Shawn, it's Vince. Open the door."

Amid a stream of obscenities, Shawn shouted through the door, "Leave me alone, Cortenza!" The sound of his lamp shattering on the ground punctuated his words.

"Shawn, it's Audrey," she tried. "Please let us in?"

The scuffle inside the office slowed, and finally, Shawn cracked open the door. He glowered when he saw the members of his force loitering in the lobby, but Vince and Audrey were quick to pull him back inside the confines of his office.

Glass was everywhere, shattered from lamps, the glass panes of his cabinets, and paperweights. His desk looked as though a hurricane had ripped through it, upending its contents all about the room. Papers were strewn in every direction.

Audrey and Vince exchanged worried looks as Shawn collapsed on the floor and leaned his head against the wall. His eyes were red and puffy, dark circles blossomed beneath them. Shawn was not one who often showed emotions, but today, it seemed like every nerve was on full display. And each of them was raw.

Vince kicked aside some broken glass on the floor and Audrey gingerly knelt beside their friend. Concern lit her features as he stared vacantly at her, his shoulders slumped in defeat. His knees were drawn to his chest, and in that moment, Shawn

Mitchel looked more like a broken toy than a tough police chief.

"Shawn, we're going to find her. You know we will," Audrey reassured him.

"Then why haven't we been able to find her, Audrey? Where the hell is my wife?" he exploded, pushing her away. "We don't have a damn lead, and she's been missing for more than twenty-four hours now. Add the fact that we have a fucking serial killer in the area, I'm losing my ever-loving mind."

"You have to stay positive, man," Vince reminded him. "Shannon is a tough woman, she's a fighter. That is something you gave her. She can make it through anything."

Shawn's eyes closed briefly as he exhaled. His dark head thumped back against the wall a few times, before he looked wearily at his friends. His wedding band caught the light and a sob choked out between his lips, leading Audrey to lean over and wrap him in her arms.

"I'm so worried she's been taken by the same psychopath we're after," Shawn cried. "That she's been a target because of me. I'm the chief of police! I should be able to protect my own wife!"

"You can't beat yourself up over this," Audrey admonished. "I'm sure Shannon is fine."

"Shawn, we are doing everything we can to find her and to stop this killer," Vince cut in. "For now, I think you need to go home. We'll call you if"—he caught the pleading look Audrey shot him—"when, not if, when we find something."

Shawn sighed and nodded miserably. The pair helped him off the ground and nearly had to hold him upright. "I'll get Anderson to drive you home," Audrey murmured.

She hurried from the room, her long blonde hair swishing against the back of her collar, searching for Officer Anderson. Audrey found him in deep conversation with Morrigan and their secretary Luna and cleared her throat to interrupt.

"Detective, is he all right in there?" Luna asked.

"Honestly, no he isn't," she replied. "But he needs us to all stay strong for him now."

"Anything we can do to help, just let us know," Roger answered.

"Actually, Anderson, I was hoping you would be able to drive him home. He's in no state to drive at present."

"Consider it done," he told her before heading to the office.

Audrey dismissed Morrigan with a tired look and headed over to where Sarah stood against the reception desk. Sarah straightened as she approached, apprehension etched in her eyes. Audrey looked as though she would topple at any moment, but the junior officer was sure if she offered support, Detective Stevens's façade would crack... and not in a good way.

"Lawson, I need you, Denise, Dr. Sheldon, and anyone else you can find to call the lab and keep on their asses about those results. We need a break, and we need it yesterday," Audrey told her. "Vince and I still need to go check in with Ellsie Lewis so we can attempt to quell the public's panic. You dogging the lab techs will be one thing we're not having to worry about as we meet with her."

"Of course, detective. I'll do everything I can and call you as soon as I learn anything," Sarah answered, forcing more bravado into her voice than she currently felt.

Vince joined them and they all watched with saddened eyes as Roger led Shawn out of the precinct. He leaned against the counter and dropped his head on his arms, feeling the weight of the case crushing his soul. Audrey laid a hand on his shoulder and his brown eyes peeked up at her, a tired smirk tugging at the corner of his mouth.

"Come on, partner," she breathed. "We've got a reporter to see."

***

When Audrey and Vince entered her office, Ellsie found her breath catching in her throat. Audrey was downright intimidating, tired as she looked, but Vince? Ellsie felt she might burn in hell for some of the thoughts running through her mind as she took in his chiseled physique, angular jaw, and thick brown hair. She lightly bit her lower lip and did her best to settle the raging inferno now burning within her.

"Please... have a seat," she stammered softly. She

brushed her red hair behind her ears, the motion catching Vince's attention.

"So, tell us what the rumor mill has right now," Audrey began, cutting right to the chase.

Ellsie sighed. "There's a lot of conflicting information from what I've gathered. They know that Monica Simpson and Kristy Hillman's deaths have been linked, but they don't know how. They also know that two more women, Shannon Mitchel and Chloe Harper, have gone missing, presumably taken by the serial killer. They have connected the dots well enough on their own to know there is someone entirely sinister targeting women."

"That's a lot for them to know right off the bat," Vince commented.

"Exactly. I'm not sure how they're getting all their information, though. No one that I've heard from has said, and when pressed, they can't give an answer on where the intel originated."

"Vince, do you think someone at the M.E. office or ours could be leaking information?"

He scratched the back of his neck thoughtfully. "I don't know, Drey. Most of them would know better, especially in a case like this, but who knows."

The three sat in silence for a moment, the only sounds coming from the ringing phones in other offices and the traffic outside Ellsie's window. Audrey was looking distractedly out at the tree beyond the glass, a small bird catching her eye. Ellsie used her preoccupation to covertly steal glances at the handsome detective next to her, only to find his warm eyes glittering mischievously back at her.

Flushing the same color as her hair, Ellsie tried to hide her embarrassment under the guise of reaching for her coffee, but it was already too late. Vince had taken note of her interested stare, and a wolfish smile twitched his mouth upward. As she bit her lip again, he ran his tongue across his own, setting her heartrate to a fever pitch.

"What should we consider releasing to the public, then?" Audrey asked, interrupting their passionate gaze.

"Um..." Ellsie said, flustered beyond belief.

"How about the basic facts, Drey? Two women are dead, two are missing. Yes, we suspect a serial killer is responsible. Be aware of your surroundings and all women should plan on going places in groups for safety," Vince answered.

How the hell is he so calm right now? Ellsie thought in amazement. She had seen the lust written in his eyes and had felt the spark arcing between them just seconds ago. It seemed impossible that Vince Cortenza would be capable of pushing aside his physical attraction in the blink of an eye.

"That sounds like the best plan," she responded, pinching the bridge of her nose.

"I can get that typed out and ready to print for tomorrow's edition," Ellsie assured them.

"Here's a thought, though," Audrey said, taking a sip from the water bottle in her hand. "What if we implemented an online tipline?"

"That's an interesting idea," Vince stated after a moment's consideration. "Ms. Lewis, can you manage something like that for us?"

"Absolutely, detectives. I can get it up and running by tonight and then post it along with the news article for tomorrow."

"Perfect," Audrey told her as she rose from her seat. "Contact us immediately if you get anything useful please."

"Of course, Detective Stevens."

Audrey walked to the door as Vince began collecting his coffee cup from the floor. With her back turned to them, he wasted no time leaning closer to the desk to wink sexily at Ellsie as he dropped his personal cell number in front of her. Shell-shocked, Ellsie Lewis was helpless to do anything besides blush as Vince followed his partner out of the office.

⸺•⸺

Monday, October 14, 2019
6:23 a.m.

Frederick Motts had been a custodian for the Outside Shakespeare Festival in Ashland for ten years. In that time, he had found countless hungover teenagers, plenty of drug paraphernalia, used condoms, and even the carcasses of deer. He considered himself a seasoned veteran of the unusual when it came to keeping the theater clean.

But as he rounded the corner of the stage that cold and crisp morning, he found himself retching in a nearby trash can. Sprawled in a heap on the ground, her lips an unearthly shade of white against her dark skin, was the body of a woman. Her eyes were open wide and bloodshot, still filled with terror. Behind her back, her arms were tightly bound. Her mouth had been kept open with an open-mouth gag designed for sexual bondage and resting in the back of her throat were a pair of dice.

Frederick shakily pulled himself together and called for the police, crying as he told them he had found Shannon Mitchel.

CHAPTER FIVE

As the sun crept over the Cascades and radiant light spilled into the outdoor theater, the stark horror of the scene was grotesquely illuminated. Custodian Frederick Motts was being seen to by a paramedic, who administered oxygen to the poor man. Audrey and Vince arrived on scene together with Sarah, a feeling of dread settling in each of their stomachs like a lead balloon.

Blake Sheldon was kneeling beside the body, carefully examining her corpse while his assistants took notes for him. Denise was hard at work photographing the scene, her kit open and ready to collect samples. As Audrey drew nearer, a gasp shuddered past her lips, tears filled her eyes, and she turned away in shock. Sarah herself was forced to rush to the nearest garbage can and heave, bile leaving a bitter taste in her throat.

Vince did his best to stand strong for his partner, pulling her into his arms and letting her sob into his chest. Despite the number of people in attendance, the theater was eerily quiet, the comments being made in whispers as they all looked at the woman they had known and admired. Shannon had been a pillar in the community at Shawn's side, and her death was already having a profound impact on them all.

"Drey?" Vince murmured against her head.

"I'm okay."

Slowly, she pushed herself out of his grasp, swiping at her eyes with the back of her hands. As she took a deep breath to settle her nerves, all eyes were drawn to the sound of a car door slamming shut. Vince rushed away from Audrey, and Henry Winters joined him, intent on keeping Shawn out of the scene.

"Shannon!" he cried as they grabbed his arms to stop him. "Oh God, no! Shannon! Let me go, you bastards! That's my wife! Shannon!"

Vince and Henry wrestled him to the ground, where he screamed, ranted, and wept. His dark eyes stared in disbelief across the lawn at the remains of his wife, Blake instructing his assistant to grab a blanket to cover her while he strode to the chief's side. Shawn struggled against Vince, but the detective held him firmly.

Blake knelt beside Shawn, partially blocking his view of the crime scene, while Denise helped Cathy spread the white sheet over Shannon. With compassion in his eyes and voice, Blake addressed Shawn to attempt to calm his distress.

"Shawn, listen to me," he said quietly. Shawn's eyes slowly rose to meet his, and Blake laid a gentle hand on his shoulder. "I know this is a devastating moment, and I wouldn't want anyone touching my wife, either, but you need to listen to me carefully. We are going to take care of Shannon with the utmost respect, and we will help you find whoever is responsible for taking her life."

Shawn broke down as Blake's word sank in. "Shawn, in order to our job as best we can, and to do right by Shannon, I need you to go home for now." Shawn shook his head as tears continued to flow, his lips twisted in agony. "Shawn, if not home, go to a hotel or to a friend's, but you can't be here. You know that. We will let you know everything we find."

Cathy approached, biting her lower lip in uncertainty. The four men regarded her inquiringly, waiting for her to break the ice. "How about I take him to the hospital to get checked out, Dr. Sheldon? He looks like he could use some fluids, and maybe something to help him rest for a bit."

"Good plan, Cathy," Blake agreed as he rose. Vince and Henry helped Shawn to his feet, supporting his weight as his strength abandoned him completely. Shawn nodded miserably and allowed them to load him into the ambulance, driving him away from the tortured remains of the love of his life.

Vince rejoined Audrey, who had remained still as a statue during the whole ordeal with Shawn, her hands clasped tightly over her mouth as tears fell silently from her blue eyes. She seemed unable to move, as if Shawn's despair had infected her as well. Blake made a comment to Henry before striding their direction.

"Detectives..."

"Blake?" Vince asked apprehensively, sensing the tone.

Blake rubbed the back of his neck nervously, eyeing Audrey's stricken face. "This is going to get very personal and very messy in about two seconds. Would it be prudent for us to call in a couple extra detectives from Medford to assist?"

"Are you saying we can't do our damn job, Blake?" Audrey snapped, jolted from her trancelike state by his suggestion.

"It isn't that at all, Audrey," he reassured her. "It's more of a 'let's focus on making sure this isn't too much for anyone' kind of thing. I don't want the teams to become overwhelmed since Shannon's death is going to hit closer to home than either of the two previous murders."

Vince ran a hand down his face in exhaustion. Silence reigned as they all considered the concept of bringing in outside detectives to assist with the case. After a long moment, Audrey looked at them both resignedly and nodded.

"You're right, Blake, that isn't a bad idea. We should call for help," she stated quietly. Vince's jaw nearly hit the ground at her words, and she rolled her eyes. "I am capable of thinking rationally, Vince."

"Contrary to popular belief," he teased under his breath.

Blake coughed as Audrey's brows rose, her mouth set in a firm line. "Vincent, take Sarah back to the precinct or home, whichever she prefers." She began walking away, only to be halted by Vince's question in her wake.

"What about you, Drey?"

Her spine was stiff, and her arms were locked at her sides as she paused. Vince could tell the moment her bravado fell as she took a deep breath to steady herself. Turning her head slightly so she could speak over her shoulder, he could see the tears streaming down her cheeks. "I'm going home for the day. I'll see you bright and early tomorrow, okay?"

Not waiting for a response, she walked off, heading for her car. Vince and Blake watched her go with heavy hearts. Despite knowing how strong of a woman Audrey was, the loss of three of her close friends, and another still missing, was sure to be crushing her very soul. Vince called dispatch to arrange for the detectives from Medford and left Blake with Roger Anderson at the scene.

Declan heard the door from the garage and looked up to find his wife standing in the doorway. Her face was pinched and her eyes downcast, making it clear the call she had received earlier had been devastating. Without a word, Audrey crossed the room to where he sat at his desk, waiting for her to tell him what she needed.

Without hesitation, she climbed in his lap and kissed him deeply, running her delicate hands through his thick brown hair. Her muscled thighs squeezed around his as she began sensually rubbing her breasts against his chest, all while his hands were still by his sides. Declan allowed her to kiss him for a few moments before sliding his hands up to grip her arms and push her back.

"Audrey, baby," he whispered as she fought to draw close again, "what's going on?"

At his softly spoken words, she sat back, and looked like a lost child. "Shannon was found this morning."

"I figured it was either her or Chloe, by the way you were acting."

"Declan, I need you to make me feel alive..." she trailed, licking her lips.

"Baby, are you sure that's what you want right now?"

"Dammit, Declan! I know what I want!" she yelled, attempting to dismount his lap. He held her firmly by the wrists, waiting for her to continue. "I want you to do every last little thing you know turns me on, makes me feel like the blood is still running through my veins."

"Oh, come on, honey, I know you have more you want to say," Declan purred, licking the pulse at her throat when she paused.

"Fine, you want me to say it?" She wrenched her wrists from his grasp to grip the back of his head, forcing his ice-blue eyes to meet her darker ones. "Declan Stevens, I hereby am demanding that you fuck my brains out all day. Is that clear enough?"

"That's exactly what I wanted to hear, baby."

He picked her up, her legs wrapping instantly around his waist, and carried her to their bedroom. Setting her on the ground he pulled his shirt over his head and tossed it on the ground while she worked on her belt. Clothes soon littered the floor until undergarments were all that remained. Declan, in his tight black boxers, picked up his lithe golden wife in her sexy lace bra and panties.

"Damn, had to wear red this morning, huh, Audrey? You know that's my favorite color on you."

Nibbling on his earlobe, she replied, "Believe me... I know. Now, I believe you are supposed to be—"

She didn't get to finish her statement as he slammed her against the wall and savagely kissed her mouth. His tongue roughly explored her mouth then retreated, leaving his teeth to graze her lower lip. Her breasts were crushed against his muscled chest, the nipples hard and erect, the lace of her bra teasing fiery trails every time he rubbed against her, allowing her to feel the power of his erection against her body.

His strong hands gripped her ass and squeezed, pinching to elicit just a hint of pain to cause the pleasure to streak through her. Declan's mouth made its way back down to her neck where he kissed and sucked, marking her skin like a brand. Audrey's nails clung to his shoulders and her breathing soon turned to moans.

A devilish smirk on his face, Declan leaned back from her neck and quickly turned to toss her on the bed. Her knees were slightly bent, and she pushed up on her elbows to smile seductively at him as he placed one knee on the bed in order to grip her panties. He ripped them off, replacing them with his hands and tongue, sending her back into the mattress in ecstasy.

"God, Declan!" she cried, gripping the covers as he pushed her over the edge into orgasmic bliss. When she opened her eyes, she was still seeing stars burst upon her sight as he quickly shed his boxers. He pulled her by the ankles closer to the edge of the bed and delighted in the gasp she made when he entered her wetness.

Declan plunged into her hard and fast, gripping her legs for maximum control. The forcefulness of his body slamming into her own left tears streaming down her face, and her head tossed on the sheet as she moaned. Soon they were both slick with sweat, and still Declan pounded her flesh.

After what seemed like hours, he finally allowed himself to release, his back arching and eyes closed in pleasure. Pulling out, he collapsed on the bed next to Audrey's quivering form. Declan draped an arm over her midriff and fondled her breast through the lacy bra.

"Was that mind-blowing enough, baby?" he teased.

"Un-huh," she whimpered, a smile tugging the corners of her mouth. "You sure know how to fuck a girl until she can hardly move, honey."

"Thank you, my love. Don't forget you were

planning to take care of the dog tonight. Do you want me to take over?"

Audrey's eyes flicked open, the dark blue orbs hard as she frowned at her husband. "I said I would do it, and you better believe I will. I need it tonight."

"Fair enough. Let me know if you want a hand, though," he said, pushing off the bed. "Are you satisfied for a bit? I need to get a contract sent really quick."

"Fine. But when you're done, be ready for round two."

"And three... and four..." Declan smirked. "Don't worry, Audrey. I promised I'd fuck your brains out all day, and that's exactly what I'll do."

With a wink, he headed back to his living room office, leaving Audrey sprawled on their rumpled bed.

Across town at the precinct, Sarah sat at the table in the layout room going over the files they had on Monica and Kristy for the twentieth time. She had refused to allow Vince to take her home yet, and instead had found herself painstakingly looking through the crime scene photographs, lists of evidence, and witness testimonies. She jotted notes on her tablet as she went, trying to find a pattern, a clue, anything that might lead to the killer.

"Any luck?" Denise interrupted, popping into the room with a couple of coffees. Sarah set her reading glasses on the table and blew on the coffee Denise offered her.

"I'm not really sure. I've been making lists and trying to connect the dots, but so far nothing is really adding up in these cases."

Denise pulled out the chair opposite Sarah and sank into the cool metal seat, her eyes never leaving the photos scattered across the table. She picked up the two sets of dice from each scene, carefully labeled, and studied them.

"We didn't collect any prints on Monica's thanks to her being in the water, and we didn't find any on the ones left with Kristy, either," she mused.

"Which leads us to believe the killer must have worn gloves at all times," Sarah agreed. "So far, there hasn't been any trace evidence in either case. With Monica, any trace evidence was corrupted by the water, and with Kristy..." Sarah sighed heavily as her sentence trailed.

"But perhaps that in itself is a clue," Denise suggested. Sarah looked up to see a light dancing in her violet eyes and raised a brow for her to continue. "No blood, hair, saliva, sweat, semen, or any other form of trace evidence from the killer points to a highly methodical killer who knows what we look for at crime scenes."

"Audrey suggested the killer was probably highly intelligent and a loner outside of the city limits." Sarah looked back at the evidence report again, a sickening feeling settling in her gut. "Denise, do you think it's possible the killer is somehow involved in law enforcement?"

"I would hope and pray not, but whoever this is has at least done their homework on the way crime scenes are processed. Maybe we're looking for a doctor or scientist, or possibly someone who flunked becoming a cop because of their psych profile."

"I suppose that would make sense. You can't become an officer or work anywhere in law enforcement if you have any form of psychosis," Sarah stated. "But what is the motive? I've been looking at both of these cases and I can't find a motive anywhere. And we need a motive or pattern to hopefully stop the next killing."

"So far, all three victims, and Chloe, too, belong to the same book club. Did you notice any other connections?"

Sarah picked up her notebook and flipped back a page. Settling her glasses back on the bridge of her nose, she began reading. "Other than the book club, let's see… all different causes of death and body dump locations, all different occupations, too. Monica and Kristy lived at the same apartment complex, but Shannon and Chloe lived in houses. Monica and Kristy were both single, Shannon and Chloe married."

"And Chloe is pregnant," Denise chimed. "God, I can't imagine what David is going through right now with her being missing."

"Yeah, no kidding."

They both looked thoughtful as they glanced at the picture of Chloe tacked to the bulletin board. Taking a deep breath, Sarah continued her run-down on the victims. "Monica was found at the base of Klamath Falls, Kristy on the Pacific Crest Trail, and Shannon at the Outside Shakespeare Festival theater. Monica was in the orchestra and taught music lessons, Kristy was the high school cheer coach, Shannon was the head of the local women's auxiliary club, and Chloe is a florist."

"You're right," Denise cut in, "they're all over the map. No wonder we haven't come up with much."

"I know Shannon and Audrey met for coffee a couple days before she went missing, and Kristy was supposedly meeting a guy the night she may have disappeared. Monica had told people she had the flu, and Chloe had gone for lunch, but no one knows where or if she went alone. I can construct a basic timeline, but that's it, Denise."

"What about these dice?" she asked, pointing the evidence baggies.

"What about them? They both have the same symbols and words on them, which is insanely odd. And each of those words means 'to die' in different languages."

"Yeah, but where did they come from? They're unusual. I know I've never seen anything like them. Someone had to manufacture them special for our killer. Maybe we can track them."

"That's not a bad idea, but I see a potential problem," Sarah commented with obvious misgivings.

"Three-D printers are becoming commonplace these days. So, anyone with basic computer software knowledge and access to one could in theory create something like this."

"Ugh, you're right," Denise admitted. "I still say it's a place to start. I can pull a couple computer techs at the lab and have them see if they can track down anyone within a hundred miles of here has purchased a three-D printer in the past six months, plus the special novelty dice manufacturers. Maybe we can get lucky with one of those avenues."

"Thanks, that will save me from the torture of the Internet," Sarah giggled. "Computers are not my friend."

"I'll go get on that now, and hopefully we can have some answers by tonight or tomorrow morning."

Denise rose and started for the door, but Sarah stopped her. "Hey, was Dr. Sheldon able to determine the type of knife used on Kristy yet?"

"All he could determine was that it was a six-inch chef knife. No other distinguishable features unfortunately. I'll let you know when we get the lab work on Shannon completed, but Blake is fairly confident she was poisoned."

"Just like on the dice we found with her," Sarah murmured.

"Yeah, makes our jobs sadistically simple when we can narrow our cause of death search thanks to a pair of fucking dice," Denise said sadly before disappearing around the corner.

At his own apartment, Vince was making his own notes about the case and checking the tip site Ellsie had created for them. She had sent him the login credentials so he could stay in the loop without constantly having to go through her. However, going through the red-headed reporter didn't seem so bad to him, either.

So far, most of what they had on the tip site was useless. They had gotten a few corroborations on last known sightings of Monica and Kristy, but little else was relevant information. Not to mention the few crackpots who had commented, claiming they knew what had happened to both murdered women, and that Shannon and Chloe had also been taken by the same entities: aliens.

"Little green men from Mars? Kill me now," he muttered in Italian. As he closed his laptop, he decided he was in desperate need of a beer.

Vince headed for his kitchen and popped a cold one open, taking a long appreciative drink. "Hell, after today, I may need something a bit stronger than one measly beer."

He went and sat on his balcony, listening to the crickets chirp as dusk approached and continued to drink sedately. Vince had always enjoyed the view his apartment offered, but today, it seemed hollow. The sun setting behind the clouds and horizon painted the landscape red, setting his nerves on edge.

He had just finished his beer and was contemplating opening another when he heard his cell ringing from inside. Sighing, he rose and picked it up, surprised to see Ellsie's name on the screen.

"Ciao, *Bellissima*," he purred in greeting.

"Um... h—hi, detective," Ellsie stammered.

Vince chuckled at her nervousness. She was an intriguing woman, one he'd love to get to know better. Perhaps when this was all behind them...

"Sorry to call you, but I thought you might want to come by my office and take a look at the latest tip I received."

"I was just looking at the tip site and didn't see anything of interest."

"No, it's not on there. My email address and number, plus yours and Detective Stevens's and the one for the precinct are all on the site. The tipster emailed me an audio clip," she corrected.

"To your personal email?"

"Work email, but yes, it came directly to me."

He ran a hand down the back of his head to his neck, fear icing through him at the implications. "Give me ten minutes and I'll be there."

"Sounds good, Vince. I'll wait for you in the lobby to let you in."

Vince followed Ellsie to her office and had to keep reminding himself not to look at her softly swaying hips or the gentle curve of her ass in the skirt she wore. The task was proving difficult. Ellsie had seemed nervous and somewhat shaken when she had called, and again when she admitted him to the office building. She quietly closed her office door after he'd entered and beckoned him to follow her to the desk.

"The email was sent anonymously, so I've been unable to trace it so far. Maybe an IT guy could have a crack at it and come up with something, though," she told him as she took her seat and began to pull up the email.

Vince leaned an arm on her desk, the scent of his cologne wafting deliciously around her. "When did the email arrive?"

"Not more than half an hour ago. I saw I had an email, I opened it, nearly lost my lunch, then called you."

"Nearly lost your lunch? What kind of email is this?" Vince asked.

"It's a chilling cry for help, Vince," she said sadly as she opened the email for him to see.

The text of the email itself was simple. "Thought David Harper might want to hear from his wife... " Below the ten words was the sound clip, and Ellsie's hand shook as she moved the cursor to click on it.

". . . Oh God, please! Please don't hurt me or the baby! I'm begging you! Let me go! I'll do anything you want, just please—NO! God, no! Get away from me! Help! Get awa—"

"*Dolce madre di dio!*" Vince cried, crossing himself in the process. "Dammit, this is bad. No wonder you almost threw up listening to this," he told her, placing a hand on her shoulder.

"Was that... was that Chloe Harper?" Ellsie gulped.

"Yeah, it was," Vince whispered. His eyes closed in an attempt to block the image her tortured voice brought to mind. "God, we cannot let David hear this recording. He will completely lose his shit."

"What about Detective Stevens?"

Vince paused as he looked vacantly at the computer screen. Audrey was hanging by a thread as it was; this might send her fully over the edge. On the other hand, she was the other lead detective on the case from their department... and Chloe's best friend. As such, she had a right to know.

"Vince?"

"Not today, Ellsie. I'll tell her tomorrow. I'll give her tonight to grieve Shannon's loss, and tomorrow she and I can dive back into hell together."

"I'm so sorry for calling you over to hear this, but I thought—"

Vince laid a finger on her lips to stop her. "You did the right thing. I'm sorry you were the recipient to begin with. They could have messaged anyone else."

As he stared into her brilliant green eyes, her lip trembled beneath his finger. Lust pounded through both of their veins despite the harrowing cry for help they had just experienced. Vince could see the pulse throbbing in her delicate neck, and impulse overtook them.

He pulled her firmly into his arms and she offered no resistance. Ellsie melted into his embrace and tilted her face up to meet his, just as his lips came crashing down upon her own. Her hands ran along the corded muscle of his back, and his tangled in her long red hair as he deepened the kiss, his tongue playfully meeting hers.

"You've been through a terrible shock tonight," he murmured into her luscious locks when he pulled back. "Are you certain you want to continue?"

Ellsie smiled up at his handsome face. "Yes," she breathed, "but not here."

"God, no, not here. Your place or mine, Miss Lewis?"

"So long as yours has a comfortable bed, that's more than fine with me."

Chuckling, Vince held onto her hand while she shut her computer down and then pulled her from her office into the night.

Tuesday, October 15, 2019
7:30 a.m.

Arriving promptly at the precinct, coffees in hand, Audrey and Vince headed directly to the layout room to meet with Blake, Sarah, Denise, and the two Medford detectives joining the team. Vince sported dark circles under his eyes, proof of his long night spent with Ellsie Lewis. He had hated to leave her asleep in his bed, but duty called. He'd left her a note and some breakfast, along with his spare key to lock up his apartment.

Audrey herself was doing her best not to let the world know how much she and Declan had been in bed, a difficult task as he had not been a gentle man yesterday. As they entered the layout room, Sarah was pulling up a slideshow she had made the day before on the computer, and Denise and Blake were going over lab results. The two visiting detectives looked up from the files they were busy perusing to greet them.

"I'm Detective Vince Cortenza, and this is my partner Audrey Stevens," he said.

"Colin Arthurs and Angela Guinabee," the tall, dark-haired man replied as they all shook hands.

"Thanks for coming down to help us," Audrey said quietly.

Angela smiled lightly at Audrey, a look of compassion filling her chocolate eyes. "We are so sorry for the losses your community has been faced with, and especially for you, as we understand the victims were all friends."

Audrey offered a thin-lipped smile in return and pulled out a chair at the table. The seven of them were soon all seated, and notes were passed around like sides at a family dinner. Denise was still waiting for reports from the IT guys on the dice, but they had checked in stating they would hopefully be done by noon.

Blake held the toxicology report for Shannon in his hands, a grim look on his face. "So, Shannon was poisoned as we suspected due to the dice; however, it took us several attempts to determine the poison."

"Was it not one routinely screened for, doctor?" Colin queried.

"Admittedly not. I was so surprised by the result I redid the test to be certain but got the same result both times."

"What was the poison?" Vince asked.

"Shannon was poisoned by a plant called *Aconitum napellus*, or more commonly, monkshood or wolfsbane," Blake answered.

"Wolfsbane? I thought that was just in legends about werewolves!" Vince exclaimed.

Audrey rolled her eyes. "Most things in legends come from real life, Vince."

"Well, yes, but... I never knew there actually was a plant called that," he defended.

"I'm not surprised, Vince," Blake told him. "Wolfsbane poisoning in the U.S. is pretty uncommon. I've rarely heard of it being used these days as a form of deliberate poisoning, but ingesting any part of the plant is deadly. And sadly, Shannon's blood and stomach both showed ridiculously high concentrations of the plant."

"How high?" Angela asked, making notes as they went.

"High enough to lead me to believe that whoever

killed Shannon is more than just sadistic. There was a certain amount of diabolical planning that went into her murder. The first bit of the poison would have caused severe vomiting, diarrhea, cramping, et cetera. It seems that Shannon's killer kept feeding it to her until she died."

"Good God!" Audrey cried, a hand flying to her mouth in shock.

"It gets worse, I'm afraid," Vince piped up. He took a deep breath, his dark eyes darting to Audrey. "Last night, Ellsie Lewis called me, stating she had received an email to her work account with a tip containing a sound clip. I met her at the office and heard the clip myself. It was Chloe Harper pleading for her life."

"What?" Audrey shrieked. "When were you planning to tell me about this, Vince?"

"Today. You didn't need to deal with it last night. I called it in to the precinct, and Ellsie forwarded the email to our IT guys to have them work on a back trace of the email it was sent from, and to see if they could come up with anything on where Chloe might be being held."

Angela nodded, having heard about the tip herself. "Have they reported back to you?"

"Not yet, although they did say it might take them up to twenty-four hours."

"Twenty-four hours? Vince, in twenty-four hours Chloe could be dead! For all we know, that clip could have been taken leading up to her murder!" Audrey practically screamed as she leapt from her seat, nearly upsetting her coffee in the process. Her blue eyes were wild, tears making them look lustrous.

Everyone at the table looked at her with sympathy; after all, Chloe was her best friend. Colin cleared his throat quietly, causing her to look his direction.

"Audrey, Angela and I both were here when the tip was forwarded and have been waiting for the report so we could act. We weren't positive if your computer experts would call him or us." He paused, looking down at the long graceful fingers of his laced hands. "That being said, we don't want to cut you out of this investigation in any form, but we would like to make two suggestions for you."

"One, is you take a step back so you're able to approach this case as rationally as possible so we can catch the killer," Angela stepped in. "And two, we would like to assign you a protective detail."

"It can't have escaped your notice that the three victims thus far, plus your friend Chloe, all belong to the same book club," Colin continued. "Medford, and a few other surrounding precincts, are organizing a team to keep watch over the remainder of your group as a precaution."

Audrey sighed as she sank back into her chair like a deflated balloon. Tears still swam in her eyes as she finally nodded miserably. "What do you want me to do now, then?"

"Right now, it might be most helpful to us if you can reach out to the other women in your club and get them all to come down to the station so we can brief them on what we're able, in an effort to equip them for what's to come," he answered.

"Audrey," Blake chimed, "he's right."

"I know," she whispered. "I'll go get to work, then."

She exited the room looking defeated, and no one could blame her for the sensation. Their backs were to a wall, and all they could do was pray they wouldn't be investigating another crime scene as a result of Chloe's cry for help.

CHAPTER SIX

Tuesday, October 15, 2019
5:36 p.m.

After a long day at the office, constantly checking the tip site for new clues, Ellsie was more than ready to call it a day. It had been grueling, writing the next segment for the serial killing story, and more so because of the chilling sound clip she'd heard the night before. A smile tugged at the corners of her mouth as she remembered the way Vince had passionately made love to her in the wee hours of the morning.

Her cell phone ringing jarred her from introspection, and she smirked as she read the name on her screen. "Were your ears burning, detective?" she purred.

"My ears? No, why?"

"Because I was just thinking about you and your very comfy bed," Ellsie giggled.

"Missing me already, *Bellissima*?" Vince asked. "That can be rectified if you'd like."

"That can be arranged. I'm about to shut down my computer for the night so I could meet you..." Her voice trailed as an instant message popped up on her screen, turning the blood in her veins to ice.

"Ellsie? You okay?"

Her mouth opened and closed in an effort to speak, but her voice was arrested as her eyes were locked on the taunting message on her computer. Ellsie could hear Vince saying her name, but she was powerless to respond. In slow motion, her hand dropped from beside her face, her phone slipped to the floor, and Ellsie felt fear grip her heart like a vise.

⸺•⸺

"Ellsie? Ellsie! Answer me!" Vince yelled through the office of the paper.

"She's in her office," a voice said from behind him.

Vince turned to find a wide-eyed beauty with pale pink streaks accenting her blonde hair. Tattoos graced her arms with detailed patterns, and nose rings winked as the light hit them.

"Who are you?" he asked gruffly.

"Alyce... I'm the photojournalist here. I help arrange the graphics for the paper."

"Sorry... just a little on edge," Vince replied. "You said she's in her office?"

"Yeah. Light is still on, meaning Lewis is probably typing away."

"Thanks!" he called over his shoulder as he sprinted toward her door.

Without knocking, he burst into her office, hand on his gun in case he needed to draw the weapon. He found Ellsie seated at her desk, tears streaming down her face, and a look of terror etched on her pale features. Vince jogged around the edge of her desk and pulled her chair to face him.

Good God, she's nearly catatonic! he realized in shock. Vince pulled her into his arms and stroked her back, trying to warm her body. His hands found their way into her red hair, and he angled her face to his.

"Ellsie? Come on, speak to me, honey."

As if awakened from her daze at last, she blinked and gazed up into his worried dark eyes. "Vince?"

"Yeah, I'm here, Ellsie. What happened?"

"I was talking with you and then... oh God, Vince! I think I'm in trouble."

"What? Why?"

"Read for yourself," she said, gesturing to the computer behind her.

Vince moved closer, his face going dark as he read the message she had been sent. The first text had been joined by many more, and each was worse than the last. Apparently, the killer felt the need to "reach out."

You never responded last night, Ms. Lewis... that's in bad taste...

Did David Harper weep when he heard his wife's cries? Something tells me he wouldn't...

Thought it time to share some insights... it's up to you to determine the full meanings...

A flute can't play if it's full of water...

Adulterers were once stoned to death for their crimes... stabbing seemed more humane...

Rumors are like poison... share them at your own risk...

The police haven't found the connection yet... have you?

Chloe is still alive... for now...

Perhaps I'll let you hear from her again tomorrow...

Sleep well, Ms. Lewis... if you can...

"Shit!" he swore, reeling back from the laptop. Vince faced Ellsie, his expression haggard. "Ellsie, you are not going to like this, but you can't be alone from now on. Clearly this killer has a mind to terrorize you, and you may potentially have a target on your back now."

"What do I need to do?" she asked softly.

"Grab your laptop. We need to take it to the precinct for analysis. Then, I'm taking you home."

Her computer chirped, signaling the arrival of another message. Together they turned to read the latest communication from the killer.

Don't waste your time with the police... they won't get anything from these messages...

"Fucking hell!"

Vince slammed her computer closed, afraid the killer may have accessed her webcam. The last thing any of them needed was for this maniac to target them. The tech guys at the precinct hadn't been able to come up with a single lead from the email she had received the night before, so clearly this killer was a tech genius.

At least that may be one more clue we can add to the profile so we can catch this fucker, he thought grudgingly.

As Vince faced her once more, he noticed her entire body was shaking. Ellsie was petrified, and rightly so considering what they had just read. He stroked her cheek, finding it cold as ice, and slowly moved to wrap his arms around her quivering form.

"Ellsie, let's get you home, okay?" he murmured. "I'll draw you a hot bath, get you some wine, and you can soak while I rub your neck."

Her green eyes rose to meet his warm gaze, and she managed the faintest of smiles. Vince led her from the office and to his car, passing a concerned Alyce on the way to the parking lot. After tucking her into the passenger seat of his car, he whipped out his cell to call Detective Arthurs at the precinct.

"Colin here."

"Colin, it's Vince. Wanted to give you a heads-up on our killer."

"What's going on, Vince?"

"He decided to reach out to the reporter tonight and was sending her taunting instant messages. He even seemed to know I was planning to take her laptop to the station because he said don't bother."

"Damn, that's not good," Colin breathed. "Is the reporter okay?"

"I'm taking her home now and will keep an eye on her for the time being. Her computer is still at her office. I'll bring it over tomorrow."

Colin sighed into the phone. "Okay, Vince, sounds like a plan. Stay sharp tonight.'"

"Copy that," Vince said, hanging up.

**Wednesday, October 16, 2019
2:13 a.m.**

Inside her black and white living room, Audrey typed furiously at her own computer, making lists to take into the precinct in mere hours. The adrenaline was pumping through her veins, making sleep impossible. She had volunteered to try to track the poison used on Shannon, as well as the gag.

Denise and Sarah were still working on the dice angle, and the other detectives were working any other evidence that surfaced, which admittedly wasn't much. Vince was charged with keeping on track of Ellsie Lewis and the tipline, plus anything else the cyber techs could give them. Copies of crime scene photos littered the glass coffee table and floor, creating a macabre scene.

"Babe?"

Audrey swiveled her blonde head to find Declan standing behind her, his ice-blue eyes looking bleary. Naked except for a pair of boxers, he stood in his leanly muscled glory, thrilling her to the core despite the task at hand.

"I didn't mean to wake you, Declan."

Dropping on the couch beside her, he gently gripped the back of her neck and massaged the tense muscles. "You didn't. I woke up and noticed you still hadn't come to bed."

"I just can't sleep, baby."

"I can always try to take your mind off of it again, Audrey," he whispered seductively. Theirs was an old game of distraction, using their lust for each other's body to push aside the stress of their jobs. It was never meant to be disrespectful in Audrey's case, but at least it gave her an outlet for the turmoil her cases could cause.

"Let me finish this last note, and then I will gladly take you up on that, Dec," she replied.

"What are you working on?"

"I'm trying to track the poison that was used on Shannon. So far, we haven't had any luck in finding private cultivators, but that doesn't mean someone didn't purchase the plant used."

"Ah... well, when you're done come to bed and I'll do some 'planting' of my own," he teased.

Audrey chuckled. "All right, you sex pest. I'll be there soon."

———◆———

9:28 a.m.

Ellsie looked haggard as she sat with Vince at the precinct, her laptop open in front of the techs. Detective Stevens walked in, looking beat herself, a brow raised as she noticed the two together.

"The killer has decided Ellsie makes for a good sounding board," Vince explained, motioning to the computer. Ellsie shivered beside him and reached for the cup of steaming coffee he had provided.

"Are you all right, Ellsie?" Audrey asked.

"Not really, but I think the shock is starting to wear off. Now I'm getting angry."

"I've got nothing, detectives," the tech announced. "Whoever this guy is, he's smart. He knows how to cover his tracks so we can't locate him.'"

"How so?" Vince questioned.

"It looks like he's using burner phones to send the emails and messages, two of them anyway, with a spoofed IP address so we can't get a lock on it. The guy knows his way around computers, that's for damn sure."

"Just freaking great," Vince sighed. "That's exactly what he said last night. Thanks for trying guys."

The two techs nodded and loaded up their bag as Sarah, Colin, and Angela joined them. Sarah's eyes went wide as she saw the messages, and she sank slowly into her chair. "This guy isn't messing around, is he?"

"Nope, he's not your typical jackass, homicidal maniac," Vince said sourly, "he's in a class all his own."

"And I'll be damned if he gets a pass on this grade," Audrey snapped. "Now, what do we have?"

"We've got a timeline worked out as best we can, and we can take a second look for the connection now that the killer has begun communicating with us," Sarah explained.

"Let's hear it, rookie," said Vince.

"Okay, so we are fairly certain Monica was

abducted sometime on Sunday, September twenty-second. Coroner put TOD late Thursday night of the twenty-sixth, and she was found at the bottom of Klamath Falls Monday the thirtieth," Sarah began, pinning notes to the board.

"Kristy was last seen by her neighbor, Barbara Snyder, after your book club Friday, October fourth, so we assume that is her probable date of abduction. Her TOD was approximately four a.m. on Tuesday the eighth, and she was found mere hours later, on the Pacific Coast Trail.

"On Friday, October eleventh, both Shannon and Chloe disappeared within hours of each other. Shannon was then found Monday morning of the fourteenth," Angela continued.

"The coroner determined her TOD to most likely have been between nine and eleven a.m. the day before," Sarah added.

"And Chloe is still missing, but according to the messages Ellsie received last night from the killer, she is still alive," Vince said.

"Let's take a look at the COD in each case real fast," Colin interjected. "Monica was drowned, as indicated via the dice with her and the water in her lungs."

"Speaking of the water in her lungs," Sarah chimed, "the lab finally got back with us on it. It wasn't the same water as is found in the falls."

"Meaning she wasn't killed there," Audrey concluded.

"Nope, it turned out to be plain, filtered water in her lungs. There was no presence of microbes one would find in water in nature," Sarah finished.

"Okay, good to know," Colin said, writing a quick note. "Kristy was stabbed with a chef knife of non-descript nature, much as one would find in any store or kitchen. Shannon was then poisoned with the obscure plant known as wolfsbane."

"That's three different CODs, and all represented by different symbols on the one die," Angela announced. "That leaves us with three other possible murders and causes available. I think it's safe to assume the shovel image means someone would be buried alive, the gun quite obviously indicates itself, as does the noose."

"I would suggest checking the registers to see who all has firearms, but let's face it, this is Oregon," Vince said tiredly. "Everyone and their brother owns a gun, and chances are they aren't all registered, anyway."

"What about recent gun purchases, and possibly rope or shovels?" Sarah asked.

"Not a bad idea, Sarah," Angela said thoughtfully, "but that still might not be much help if the killer bought his supplies months in advance."

"This is a damn nightmare," Vince growled. "We've got no leads, no suspects in every case, hardly any evidence, and this prick is taunting us. Some detectives we are, huh?"

They all exchanged weary looks, and Audrey's lips pursed into a thin line. Every one of them was becoming discouraged with the lack of progress on the case, and it was igniting a sense of desperation. A timid cough caused them all to turn to the red-headed reporter.

"What if..." Ellsie began, pausing to close her eyes and take a deep breath. "What if I tried to reach out in return?"

"Have you lost your fucking mind?" Vince exploded.

"Believe me, I'm not looking forward to this, but the killer already seems to want to talk with me, so maybe I could get him to communicate more. Possibly learn something new that traditional methods wouldn't provide."

Looking thoughtful, Colin rubbed his chin. "It's not a horrible idea, although I'm quite certain it will be a traumatizing task, Ms. Lewis. Are you confident you can manage the stress?"

"Honestly, I don't know. But I do know that I have this opportunity to do something that might help."

"Ellsie..." the groan slipped from Vince's lips, his eyes looking pained.

"Let me do this, Vince," she replied, laying a hand on his bicep to calm him.

Angela cleared her throat, drawing their eyes back to the group. "For now, I say it can't hurt for Ms. Lewis to try to reach out to the killer so long as she follows some simple safety protocols. For instance, you have an officer guarding you at all times."

"I'll keep on that," Vince answered.

"Fine. Make sure you alert us if you learn anything. Also, I think it would be wise if she refrained from going to her usual locations, such as home or work. Would you have a problem with her staying with you, Vince?"

"No, that's fine," he told Angela.

"Good. We'll let you two go and get your arrangements settled then," Colin dismissed them. "The rest of us need to keep working on any possible lead we can find. Audrey, it might be helpful if you went over witness testimonies again, see if we missed something."

"Okay, I can do that, Colin. Do you mind if I do that at home? I can spread everything out better there and focus more."

"Go for it."

Audrey followed Vince and Ellsie to the parking lot, watching her partner help the other woman into his car. He smiled grimly and waved, and she took a deep breath before returning the gesture. Heading for her own car, she adjusted the strap of her bag on her shoulder, laden with files and documents to study.

This is going to be a long night, she thought.

⸺ ◆ ⸺

Sitting in the passenger seat of Vince's Mustang, Ellsie squirmed nervously. She knew he was not happy with her idea, but she also didn't care. She had to do what she felt was right. It was the reason she had gotten into journalism: to tell the truth and help those in her community.

I don't care if he doesn't like this idea, but I do care that he isn't mad at me, she thought as she twirled her hair around her finger. She bit her lower lip, wondering if she should break the ice between them, but Vince beat her to it.

"Just so you know, I think you're very brave for volunteering to this. Brave, but I won't lie to you and say I'm happy about it. I'm terrified this is going to rebound horribly and you're going to get hurt."

"And that would upset you?" she asked quietly.

Vince pulled the car off the road and parked, turning to face her. He brushed a strand of hair behind her ear and smiled at her. "Yeah, Ellsie, it would upset the hell out of me if something happened to you. I know I have a reputation for being a player, and honestly, I am one. But I am faithful to the girls I sleep with for the time I sleep with them. And I don't tend to sleep with random girls unless we have a connection. I felt it the first time we met, and I think you did, too."

Ellsie blushed, a sizzling sensation running through her entire body. His words excited her, calmed her, and ignited a passion within her. "I felt it, Vince," she whispered.

In the next instant, Vince was claiming her mouth with his own, his hands gripping the sides of her face as he deepened the kiss. Reluctantly, he broke away from her a moment later, looking at her with big puppy-dog eyes. "As much as I would love to lay the seat down and go at it right here," he started, making her giggle, "I really don't want my own fellow officers to write me up for indecent exposure. So, what do you say we run by your place so you can grab a few things and then head back to my apartment?"

"I say, drive fast, detective," she purred in his ear.

"Yes, ma'am."

———•———

Audrey arrived home to find Declan on a conference call, so she quietly made her way to their sunroom. She set down her bag before heading to their room to change her clothes. Five minutes later, she returned in comfy yoga pants, a tank top, and her hair pulled back. She curled up on the divan and pulled the first transcript from the bag.

"The following is the interview with David Harper, husband to Chloe Harper, conducted by Sarah Lawson on Saturday, October 12th at 10:30 a.m. Mr. Harper, when was the last time you spoke to your wife?"

"Yesterday morning before we both left for work," David replied.

"That was the 11th; around what time?"

"I left at 7:30 like I do every weekday."

"Do you know what your wife's plans for the day were?"

"Chloe opens her shop at 9 a.m. Monday through Friday, and she usually arrives around 8:30 to set everything up beforehand. Yesterday was no different.

She usually breaks for lunch around noon, and closes at 5 p.m. She had mentioned she was meeting someone for lunch."

"Did she happen to say who she was meeting?"

"No, just someone from the book club."

"I see. Who all works with your wife at her shop?"

"Just her assistant, Liliana."

"Is it true that Fridays are when her book club meets?"

"Yes, but Chloe wasn't sure they were going to have it last night due to Monica and Kristy being dead. She's also been more tired since becoming pregnant, so she's missed a few nights due to that. Bridget Middleton, the president, hasn't been too thrilled with her."

"Do you know if she was planning to attend if they were having the meeting?"

"I don't. She's been playing it by ear the past few months. If she has a slow day at the shop and feels like it, she goes. Otherwise, she chooses to stay home."

"And what is your relationship like with your wife?"

"My relationship? What do you mean by that?"

"It's just a question, Mr. Harper."

"It sounds more like an accusation."

"We're just trying to have a greater understanding of your wife, sir. We want to bring her home safely."

David sighed heavily. "I love Chloe, believe me, I do. But I won't lie and say we have the perfect marriage. Here lately, there's been added stress because she's pregnant."

"How so?"

"She owns her own business and is only one of two employees. When she gets further into her pregnancy, she may not be able to work as much, not to mention when the baby arrives. I'm stressing over our finances."

"And remind me what you do for a living, Mr. Harper?"

"I work at the bank as a loan officer."

"The one Elijah Middleton runs?"

"Yeah, that's correct. That's how Chloe ended up in the book club, actually."

"What do you mean?"

"Elijah's wife is Bridget, so she and Chloe met at a bank function. I initially hated the idea because at the time, Bridget's group met at his house instead of the bookstore."

"Why would them meeting at his house be a cause for concern?"

"Because Elijah has eyes for other women, especially if they're attractive. Bridget is a conniving shrew of a woman, and he would divorce her if it were financially beneficial to him. Unfortunately, Bridget comes from serious money, so he won't."

"Meaning he likes to flirt with other women in the meantime?"

"Pretty much. He's commented on Chloe's appearance more times than I can count in the three years I've worked for him. I don't say anything to him about it because I want to keep my job. But I do know that he spends a ridiculous amount of money at her shop buying flowers for that bitch he calls his wife."

"Really?"

"Yeah. My personal opinion is he does it just so he can see Chloe."

"Do you think there's any chance he and Chloe may have been having an affair?"

"Don't you think that crossed my mind? Chloe wouldn't have the nerve to cheat on me. She wouldn't be able to keep it a secret. And I happen to know, thanks to Bridget's gossipy nature, that if Elijah is ever caught cheating on her, he gets nothing in the divorce."

"Very interesting. One final question for you: can you think of anyone who may have wanted to harm your wife, or even you?"

"Other than Bridget, and only because she's a bitch, no."

"Okay, thank you for your time, Mr. Harper, you were very helpful."

"Please... find my wife."

"We're doing everything we can, sir."

Declan poked his head into the sunroom to check on her once his call was over. She smiled up at his tanned face and tilted her mouth up to meet his. "Hi there."

"Hi back," she giggled. "How was your call?"

"Oh, you know, crazy investors who think they own the world. Same as usual," he laughed. "What are you working on?"

"Reading through the witness testimonies again to see if we missed something the first time."

Declan looked at her with raised brows. "Isn't that kind of a Hail Mary for you?"

"Yeah, but at this point in time, we have no leads."

"Not even from that tipline you suggested?"

"Oh, the reporter has been getting more than she bargained for with it, but nothing of much use just yet. Everyone at the precinct is still stumped and is calling the killer a tech genius."

"Really, now?"

"Yep. Now, as much as I would love to keep talking, Declan, I have to get back to work."

"I'll see you later to make sure you eat," he told her as he stood and kissed her cheek.

Once he had left the room, Audrey pulled the next transcript from the bag, this one detailing the conversation with Chloe's business partner, Liliana.

"This is the interview with Liliana McCoy, conducted by Officer Sarah Lawson on Saturday, October 12th at 1:00 p.m. Ms. McCoy, you work with Chloe Harper, correct?"

"Liliana or Lils is fine, and yes, I've worked with Chloe for about ten months now."

"Liliana, you phoned Chloe's husband, David, yesterday to tell him she had not returned from a lunch meeting, correct?"

"Yes, that's correct. Chloe left the shop around noon as she always does, and so did I, and usually we both return around 1 p.m. I got back from lunch early, and just assumed I beat her. When she didn't return by 1:30, I started getting worried."

"And was that when you called David?"

"No, first I tried calling Chloe half a dozen times. And when I couldn't reach her, and she still hadn't come back by nearly 3 p.m., I called him."

"Do you happen to know who she was having lunch with yesterday?"

"Not a clue. I assumed it was someone from her book club, but she never said."

"Okay, final question, Liliana. Can you think of anyone who would want to harm Chloe?"

"God, no. Chloe is the sweetest person ever. She puts up with my dramatic ass every day, and I have no clue how she does it."

"Okay, well, if you think of anything else, please give us a call."

"Of course. I hope you find her soon."

——•——

The final transcript she had brought home was a two-part interview with Bridget and Elijah Middleton. Audrey bristled at the thought of Bridget since the two of them tended to butt heads during book club meetings. Bridget was an entitled bitch in Audrey's opinion. In fact, she had only agreed to join the group at Chloe's insistence.

"The following is the interview with Bridget Middleton—"

"That's Mrs. Bridget Middleton to you!"

"My apologies, ma'am. The interview with Mrs. Bridget Middleton as conducted by Officer Sarah Lawson on Sunday, October 13th at 3 p.m. Mrs. Middleton, what can you tell me about Chloe Harper?"

"Chloe is a foolish girl, if you ask me. Getting herself pregnant like that."

"Pregnant like what, Mrs. Middleton?"

"Just pregnant, officer. Children are a waste of time and resources. And as soon as that baby came, Chloe would have been kicked out of my book club."

"And why is that, ma'am?"

"Because she would have insisted on bringing the baby with her, or she would miss too often to still be considered a member. That's why."

"There's no need to be so hostile. What was your relationship like with her?"

"As I said, she was a foolish girl. I only agreed to allow her into the club because my husband insisted it would be good for her to make more friends. More friends, my ass. He just wanted her to be around more often. I took care of that problem quick enough."

"Took care of the problem? How?"

"We stopped meeting for the club at our house within two weeks of Chloe joining. I refused to allow my husband's wandering eyes to linger on her every time she came over."

"And did your husband ever make a move on Chloe?"

"You're kidding, right? If Elijah ever so much as touches another woman, he'll find himself divorced and broke faster than he can say 'hello.'"

"It sounds like you have a lot of pent up rage where Chloe is concerned. Is that a fair assessment?"

"Rage is a strong word, officer. I wasn't her biggest fan, but believe me, I had nothing to do with her disappearance. It doesn't benefit me at all. Chloe knew her place, so I had no reason to hurt her."

"Interesting."

"Are we done here?"

"As soon as I speak with your husband, yes. But you're welcome to go wait in the lobby."

"Fine, I'll send Elijah in to speak with you."

"Thank you, Mrs. Middleton."

"I thought you just needed to speak to my wife, detective," Elijah stated.

"It's officer, actually. Officer Sarah Lawson, conducting the interview with Elijah Middleton. Mr. Middleton, how well did you know Chloe Harper?"

"Call me Elijah, sweetheart, and I knew Chloe as well as some, I guess."

"Could you elaborate on that, please?"

"Chloe is my loan officer's wife, so I met her through him at a work function. She then began attending my wife's book club."

"I heard that you are a frequent customer at her floral shop as well."

"Yeah, I go in there to buy flowers for Bridget at least once a week. Chloe always does a great job arranging the flowers, so I figured I'd support one of my own's family."

"Any truth to the suggestion you had your sights set on Chloe romantically?"

"Officer, I'm a married man. Chloe is an attractive woman, yes, but I'm committed to my wife. I'm sorry if David got the wrong impression by some of my comments. They were only meant to be encouraging to him since he seemed so down about her pregnancy lately."

"I see. And what do you know about their relationship?"

"David and Chloe? Oh, well, Chloe is a very affectionate woman, and David is a fairly private man. She's bubbly and he's uptight. But they clearly love each other and make a charming couple in spite of their differences."

"Do you know if they were having any problems?"

"Not really. Chloe has always been so cheerful every time I speak with her, and David doesn't really confide in me."

"Do you know of anyone who would want to cause Chloe harm?"

"No. Like I said, Chloe is always cheerful and smiling. She's an absolute sweetheart. Why anyone would want to hurt her is beyond me."

"Okay, Mr. Middleton, I think we're done here."

"Let me know if you need anything else please, Officer Lawson."

"Wow, Elijah was laying on the charm extra thick

that day. Poor Sarah," Audrey chuckled, setting the report back in the file.

As she looked at the remaining transcripts to read, a hopeless realization sparked within her mind. It didn't seem to matter how many people they interviewed, the number of times they ran the evidence, or how they looked at the case. They still had their backs to the wall and no leads.

CHAPTER SEVEN

Wednesday, October 16, 2019
8:11 p.m.

Inside the brightly painted walls of his kitchen, Shawn sat on the floor, surrounded by empty liquor bottles. The sun had long since faded beyond the horizon, reminding him of his life with Shannon. They'd had so many plans for the future, but like the light of day, they had vanished the moment her lifeless body had been found.

After being discharged from the hospital, Shawn had made his way to the local liquor store and stocked up on all manners of booze. The thought of returning to their home knowing Shannon would never again walk through the front door and instantly brighten his life with her exuberant personality was enough motivation to drink his weight in alcohol. Shawn's eyes rose blearily from the floor to look at the orange walls and stainless-steel appliances around him.

Shannon loved all things bright, he thought miserably. She had been bursting with life and had begged him to allow her to paint the walls to remind her of the autumn leaves.

"Come on, Shawn! It'll be so fun to have a unique kitchen like this," she had exclaimed at the hardware

store. "*You know how much I love walking through the woods in fall, and this color perfectly reflects that concept!*"

"*I get that, but orange? How will that color not give you a headache when you cook?*"

"*You clearly have no imagination, honey. Have no fear; Shannon is here to help you broaden your horizons and embrace the vitality of life!*"

That had been last year. Shawn took the final swig from the bottle in his hand as he glowered at the walls Shannon had lavished her personal style upon. Rage flooded his mind and he threw the bottle at the wall, watching it shatter on the floor.

Despair filled him, and he dropped his head into his hands and wept. Everyone assumed Shawn was the strong one in the relationship since he was a cop. The truth of the matter was, Shannon was the one who had the heart and mind of steel. She carried him and helped him in ways he hadn't even known he needed.

The thought that they would never have children together, never watch another movie curled together on the couch, never laugh and tease one another while cooking at the stove, never fall asleep and wake in each other's arms was a devastating weight pressing down upon him. Shannon had wanted a dozen children when they first married; Shawn had talked her down to three or four. She wanted to travel and learn a third language.

Shawn had been looking forward to their upcoming anniversary trip he had planned in secret for her. Shannon had always loved New York, and he had bought the plane tickets, booked the hotel, and arranged for tickets to a show on Broadway months ago. He was going to spoil her with all sorts of shopping and tourist-type activities and tell her that weekend that he was finally ready to try for their first child.

None of it would happen now.

"God, Shannon! What the hell am I supposed to do without you?" he yelled while sobbing. The cool metal of his wedding band seemed to burn his temple, causing his tears to fall harder than before. "Shannon..." he murmured. "Shannon, come back to me..."

⚊⚫⚊

Thursday, October 17, 2019
5:30 a.m.

Audrey woke early and carefully eased out of bed to keep from waking Declan. She donned her robe and quietly walked downstairs, intent on reviewing the testimonies again, along with all the crime scene photos. As she entered the living room, she could hear the whining, but chose to ignore it for the time. She would see to the matter later.

Quickly twisting her hair back from her face, she hit the button to start the coffee machine before spreading profile pictures across the counter. Some were the victims they knew of so far, and some were witnesses, family, or possible suspects. Audrey rubbed her temple as she waited for her caffeine to be ready and set her notepad and pen before her.

"Okay," she started as she spoke softly to herself, "we've got Gregory Daniels as a person of interest in both Monica and Kristy's cases since he was their landlord and had a thing for Kristy apparently. But he doesn't really seem to fit the profile unless he's a brilliant actor."

Rolling her eyes as she thought back to the interview she and Vince had conducted the day Kristy had been found, Audrey highly doubted that possibility. *Guy looked like he was going to piss his pants. Didn't exactly scream mass murderer.*

Audrey's blue eyes focused on the picture of Bridget. There was no denying Bridget was a controlling bitch, but she hated getting her hands dirty. She did, however, have plenty of money to throw around. "What if she thought Elijah was involved with them? I know she thought he flirted with Chloe, and according to the others in the book club, Kristy was supposed to be meeting with a married guy the night she disappeared. Could it have been Elijah, and Bridget found out?"

Deciding the Middletons would make for a good jumping-off point, Audrey poured herself a cup of coffee and continued to make notes. An hour later, she had a couple pages worth of neatly written observations when Declan snaked his arm around her waist and kissed her cheek.

"Morning, baby girl."

"Morning, Declan. Coffee should still be warm if you want some," she said, not looking up.

"I'm good, but thanks. How's it going?"

"I think I may have found something, but it's flimsy at best. Maybe Ellsie will get lucky and the killer will contact her today with some more clues."

"Do you think the killer will communicate with her?"

Audrey's blue eyes rose to meet his own. "I'm hoping he does. We need something else, and as much as I hate to say this, it must come from the killer. He seems to want to talk with her, so let's have them both be useful."

"Well, I hope you get exactly what you want, baby," he said with a grim smile.

"Don't I always?"

8:29 a.m.

At Vince's apartment, Ellsie had also slipped from the bed they'd shared the night before and had been waiting at her laptop for nearly an hour. She had posted a small blurb on the tipline website asking the killer to reach out to her once again. Either he didn't check it often, or he wasn't going to show. Ellsie wasn't sure which scenario she preferred.

Vince was busy in the kitchen, making them a late breakfast and another round of coffee. He was shirtless, just in a pair of basketball shorts, flipping pancakes with ease. Ellsie decided she could happily sit and watch him forever. Tucking a rogue wisp of hair behind her ear, she found his eyes sparkling at her before giving her a devilish wink.

Ellsie giggled and blushed, trying to determine how to respond to his overt flirtation when her laptop pinged, signaling the arrival of an email. Assuming it was Sam or Alyce checking in, Ellsie clicked on the message without pause. When it materialized on her screen, she felt her skin grow clammy and her heart begin to race.

"Vince..." she murmured.

His brown eyes quickly saw the change in her demeanor, and he rushed to her side. The images on her screen caused his eyes to widen in shock. Pictures of Chloe Harper abounded, showing her shackled to some sort of basement wall. It honestly looked like a gothic dungeon with a dirt floor, rock walls, and iron bars.

Tears coursed down Chloe's cheeks, evident from the grime coating her fair skin. Her clothes appeared tattered and stained, her hair greasy, and the terror in her eyes was enough to make the hardened detective feel the cold grip of fear. Ellsie closed her eyes briefly, seeming to pray over the missing woman, then bit her lip as she continued to scroll through the pictures.

Each image was time-stamped, letting them know Chloe had been alive at least at midnight the night before. As Vince looked closer on a picture Ellsie had clicked on, he pointed out what appeared to be the tell-tale shadow of a noose behind her. Clearly her captor was tormenting her with the proposed method of her demise.

They were both distracted by the smell of smoke emanating from the kitchen. Their eyes swiveled, only to realize Vince had left some pancakes cooking on the griddle when he had come to her side, causing them to burn.

"Damn it!" he cried, jumping to dump the burned flapjacks in the sink.

As he glared at the steaming mess in his sink, Ellsie stared at him. When his eyes met hers in frustration and embarrassment, Ellsie lost it, and began laughing hysterically.

"Ellsie? What the hell could be so funny right now?"

"It's just…" she wheezed as she continued to laugh. "Burned pancakes… oh my…"

Vince watched her in fascination for a moment as tears began slowly leaking from her eyes as she laughed. Finally, it dawned on him. He had gotten so upset over burned pancakes when they were being sent pictures of a captive woman who was likely going to die soon unless they found her. It was utterly ridiculous.

A tense smile broke out on his face as he felt the hysteria reaching his brain as well. Shaking his head, Vince brought a plate of pancakes and syrup over to the table and waited for Ellsie to wipe the tears from her face and join him. As they sat down together, Ellsie smiled sadly at him.

"What are you thinking?"

With a sigh, she replied, "That this case is becoming so overwhelming. My brain obviously agrees, hence the crazed laughter."

"Well, you know what they say," Vince answered. "If you didn't laugh, you'd cry."

"And at least it reminds me I'm still alive."

Vince squeezed her hand gently where it rested on the table. When her eyes finally met his, he nodded his dark head in agreement.

"Yes, laughter does tend to signify we're still alive," he told her. "But there are other ways to accomplish that goal, Ellsie."

His voice had lowered to a seductive purr and his thumb lightly brushed the top of her hand, igniting a fire within her body. Suddenly shy, Ellsie bit down on the corner of her lip and blushed. Vince's hands were soon threading through her red hair and his lips claimed hers in a passionate kiss.

Breakfast forgotten, and thankfully the killer as well, he led her back to his bedroom and eased her back onto the mattress. Her conscience nagged at her, telling Ellsie this was in poor taste considering the images the killer had just sent her. Her body didn't align with those notions and filled with traitorous heat as Vince's muscled body hovered above her.

As Vince's lips grazed her soft neck in a whisper of a kiss, Ellsie whimpered from the pleasure coursing through her veins. She could feel his mouth turn up in a smirk against her skin and ran her fingers down his back, pulling him closer still. Just before the atmosphere turned insatiably intimate and clothes were about to fly, Ellsie's cell phone rang from the other room.

"Ignore it, baby," Vince murmured.

"I wish I could. I promised I would answer it."

Crawling out from under him, Ellsie scurried to the living room and picked up the call just before it went to voicemail. "Ellsie Lewis."

The voice on the other line was chilling with the help of the computerized alteration, and Ellsie found herself dropping onto the sofa in fear.

"Ms. Lewis, I thought I explained to you it was rude to not reply to my messages," the ambiguous voice stated. "And here I was nice enough to send you an email this morning in response to your memo. For shame, Ellsie."

"What do you want from me?"

"I believe you reached out to me first, Ms. Lewis. I'm assuming you told the police you would attempt to communicate with me to learn some valuable information about me. I hate to disappoint, but I don't plan to make things that simple for you."

Ellsie's blood turned to slush as the killer spoke, his cadence perfectly measured despite the voice-altering device. She could practically feel the evil oozing through the phone to envelop her body with every word he said. Forcing herself to take several deep breaths, Ellsie gripped her phone with white knuckles, praying she would have the courage to keep talking.

"Answer this, then, please," she said in a voice that reverberated with fear. "Is Chloe Harper still alive, right at this moment?"

The killer laughed, the noise disturbing even with the mechanical sound of it. "She was when I sent you those pictures, Ms. Lewis."

"That's not an answer to my question."

"Look at you, getting bold with a murderer," the killer taunted. "It's nice to see Detective Cortenza has been able to strengthen your spine in the past twenty-four hours."

"How do you know—"

"How do I know you're with Cortenza? I know more than you could possibly comprehend. As for Chloe, I'll throw you a small ray of hope. Yes, she's still alive. Though I can tell you this, Ms. Lewis. If I don't kill her, David Harper will."

"Why do you say that?" Ellsie gasped in horror. "From everything I know about them, David loves his wife desperately."

"Loves her, yes. Would be tolerant and forgiving if he knew the truth about Chloe. I don't think so."

"What do you mean? You clearly want to tell me something, so please answer that," she begged, loathing the desperation in her voice.

"Let's just say this: David Harper is not a man who

typically enjoys leftovers. And he isn't the only man in town to believe the statement, 'if you didn't like it the first time, you won't like it a second time'. His darling little wife had a secret from several people, and the truth would destroy so many."

"What secret?"

"I've already given you an enormous lead, Ms. Lewis. I suggest you use your brain and decipher my clue. I'll be in touch."

"Wait, I still—" Ellsie began, only to hear the click of the other line as it went dead. She sat on the couch staring at the phone in her hand as though it were a viper, waiting to strike. *What had the killer meant about giving her a clue?*

"Are you all right?" Vince asked quietly from beside her.

Still dazed, she shook her head, sending her red hair into her face. Brushing the strands behind her ear, Vince pulled her into his arms as she wept.

10:02 p.m.

Hours later, Vince and Ellsie were curled up on his sofa, doing their best to watch television and not think of the horrifying email and phone call she had received earlier. Night had fully fallen across Ashland, the waning full moon shining down upon the sleepy town. With the lights turned down, Ellsie jumped in terror when Vince's phone suddenly came to life.

Quickly pausing the movie, Vince grabbed his phone and stared at it with a slight frown. "Hello?"

"Vince? Oh thank, God," a female voice floated through the line.

"Emily, what's going on?"

Ellsie raised a brow in question but wisely kept quiet. She found herself inexplicably jealous, a feeling that was completely foreign to her.

"Vince, I really hate to call, but I swear someone is lurking outside my building! And what with the murders going on, I just got really scared. Please, could you come check it out?"

Vince sighed. "Emily, that's what 911 is for."

"I know, but you could be here so much faster," the girl pled. "Please, Vince?"

Glancing at Ellsie, Vince sighed heavily once more. "Okay, fine. Give me a couple minutes and I'll be there."

"Oh, thank you!"

As he hung up the phone, Ellsie offered him a weak smile. "Old girlfriend?"

"Something like that." He rose, tucking his phone into his pocket as he did. "Ellsie, I don't want to leave you here, but I am certainly not taking you with me to check this out. I shouldn't be more than twenty minutes or so, okay?"

"I understand, Vince," she answered, running her tongue along her bottom lip like her mouth suddenly went completely dry.

Vince leaned down and kissed her cheek before grabbing his gun and keys. Ellsie watched as he shut the door behind him, and the lock clicked into place. Hugging herself to stay warm against the sudden chill within, she paced in the living room.

After ten minutes, her phone vibrated on the coffee table. Without checking the screen, she answered, assuming it would be Vince calling to tell her he was coming back. Instead, she was met with the computerized voice of the killer.

"Ms. Lewis, would you like the chance to play the heroine tonight?"

"What do you mean?"

"What would you do if I told you could come pick Chloe Harper up and take her home, but only if you came alone?"

Ellsie gulped hard as she realized what he was offering. The chance to rescue Chloe was a tempting offer, but to do it alone, wouldn't that be suicide?

"Tick tock, Ellsie. I'm not a patient person. The offer expires in ten seconds. Do you want the location or not?"

Heart hammering in her chest, she took a deep breath and answered, "Yes."

"Good girl. Now here's what you're going to do. You're going to leave Vince Cortenza's apartment in the next sixty seconds once this call is completed. Then you will walk, and I suggest quickly, to the alley behind First National Bank. That shouldn't take you more than five minutes. Wait there, and I will deliver Chloe to you."

"Okay, I can do that."

"And Ellsie," the electronic voice hissed, "leave your phone. If you fail to comply with any of my instructions, Chloe Harper will be killed, and I'll personally leave her on your doorstep."

The phone clicked in her ear, leaving Ellsie in shock. There was no time to think, and she bolted for the door. As she neared, she noticed an unopened bag of chips sitting on the table. She smashed the chips inside and cut the corner off the bag before hurrying outside.

With every step she took, crumbs shifted out of the bag, forming a trail behind her. She could only hope that Vince returned soon and saw it because she feared she would need his help.

10:20 p.m.

When Vince returned from Emily Cross's apartment building, he was seething with frustration. There hadn't been anyone about, although there was certainly evidence to suggest someone had been lurking in the bushes prior to his arrival. He hadn't wanted to leave Ellsie and yet he'd done it... for no real reason.

Approaching his door, his hand flew to his hip when he noticed the portal was ajar. He knew for a damn fact he had shut and locked it when he left. Slipping his weapon from the holster, Vince shouldered the door open, swinging his gun around the room.

Ellsie was nowhere to be seen. "Ellsie? Damn it, where the hell are you?"

Something crunched under his feet as he moved toward the coffee table where her phone lay. *Potato chips?* his mind screamed as his saw the crumbs. Grabbing her phone, Vince flicked it open to reveal her call log. His heart sank into his stomach when he saw the entry made four minutes earlier... from an unknown caller.

"Son of a bitch!" he raged.

As he turned toward the door once again, he noticed the trail of crumbs leading outside. His eyes flashed to the table, remembering he had a new bag on the table. It was gone. *Atta girl, Ellsie!* Vince clicked his flashlight to life and raced out the door, following her trail of crumbs.

10:27 p.m.

Where is he? Ellsie thought nervously. She had arrived moments before, having nearly run from the adrenaline rushing through her body. A few doors down from the bank, she had ditched the chip bag, now empty, so as not to alert the killer of her plan. She could only hope he hadn't seen her leave the apartment with it.

She looked at her watch, the time glowing ominously in the dark. She had made it on time, but he wasn't there, and neither was Chloe. Ellsie had even checked in the dumpster to be certain. She twirled her hair around her finger as the anxiety built within her to staggering new heights.

Just when she was beginning to think this was all a scam, a car rumbled into the alley, its headlights pinning her in place. It was stopped, the engine revving menacingly as she stared. The driver was a mere hazy silhouette, the headlights blinding her to anything else.

Then everything shifted in the blink of an eye. The car lurched forward, barreling toward her at a terrifying speed. Ellsie was frozen in fear, unable to move her legs to carry her to safety. She heard a shout, then felt the force of a powerful body rushing at her to push her out of the way. Together their bodies crashed onto the unforgiving pavement just as the car exploded into the wall.

"Ellsie! Talk to me!"

She recognized the voice as Vince after a moment, though she was too dazed to speak. Her eyes were transfixed on the mangled remains of the sedan behind him, and the blood seeping from the driver's side door. Vince ran his hands up to her cheeks and forced her eyes to meet his.

"Ellsie? Can you hear me?"

"Vi-nce," she finally managed. Her voice was weak, barely more than a whisper, her green eyes luminescent with unshed tears.

Vince pulled her into his arms, causing her to cry out in pain. He shone his flashlight along her arm only to find a jagged cut dripping blood to the ground. "Damn, I am so sorry, Ellsie."

"It's not your fault, Vince," she tried to reassure him as the sound of sirens drew near.

"It may not be, but I still feel horrible. I never should have left you alone," his dark brown eyes flashed as he looked at her. "And what the hell were you thinking by coming here alone?"

"I had to, Vince," Ellsie cried. "He told me I could save Chloe if I came here. Otherwise he would kill her and dump her on my doorstep. I had to come! I just had to, Vince!" Her voice rose with each sentence, the pain bursting forth like a dam whose walls had just collapsed.

"Hey, easy, easy," Vince told her, slowly rubbing calming circles on her back. "I'm sorry I snapped at you. I was just so worried. Thank God you left that trail of crumbs. Otherwise, I might not have made it in time."

Ellsie simply nodded, causing millions of stars to burst on her sight. She winced as she slowly ran her uninjured hand up to feel the back of her head. Vince glanced behind at the crashed car and drew his gun. Walking closer, he kept the gun trained on the driver's head.

Opening the door, Vince grimaced, smelling the tell-tale sign of death escaping the vehicle. He pushed the driver back and sketched a quick cross over his chest at the sight. The driver's forehead was split open, revealing a deep crack in the skull that ran all the way down to his mouth. The guy looked like a sledgehammer had been taken to his face.

Police cars, a fire truck, and ambulance were all suddenly on scene, and Vince helped carry Ellsie to the ambulance for the paramedics to look her over. Knowing she was in good hands, he stepped over to the other officers to relay what he knew about the evening to them. He quickly gave his statement and promised to bring Ellsie to the station first thing in the morning so she could give hers.

Roger Anderson motioned him to the side before he left and nodded his head at the grisly scene behind them. "Vince, do you think we got lucky tonight and that's our serial killer?"

"I would love to say yes, Roger, especially since the killer is the one who called Ellsie and told her to be here, but something tells me it's not. I can't explain it, but I get the feeling that's not him."

"I was afraid you would say that," the other man said exhausted. "Thanks for your help tonight, Vince. I'll let you know what we find."

"Sounds like a plan," he called as he walked briskly to the ambulance.

Inside the well-lit cabin, Ellsie was laying on the stretcher, two paramedics working to get a temporary bandage on her arm and intravenous fluids started. They looked up as he approached.

"Hey, detective," Josh greeted. "We're going to be

taking her to the hospital as soon as we finish here."

"And from the look of you, I'd say you need to come as well," Cathy told him, looking Vince up and down. "Hop in and we'll give you a lift."

"Thanks, guys."

Minutes later, the ambulance pulled away from the scene, making room for the coroner's van to arrive. Vince knew it was going to be a long night for everyone involved.

⚊⚊•⚊⚊

Friday, October 18, 2019
6:47 a.m.

After her last run had ended with her terrifying discovery of Kristy Hillman on the Pacific Coast Trail, Zoey Bonall had decided to take a different path. Dawn was barely pearling the sky a soft pink as she jogged through Lithia Park, very aware of the fact she was the only one there.

Nerves started setting in as she neared the Atkinson Bridge, but Zoey did her best to push them aside. She was determined to keep running, even if the fear still existed. The crisp morning air burned in her lungs as she crossed the bridge and headed down the trail by the water.

As she paused by the bench to catch her breath, she made the mistake of turning around. Zoey nearly stumbled backward over the bench as she scrambled to get away. Screams, raw and devastating, ripped from her mouth and shattered the quiet of the morning.

Zoey's hazel eyes could hardly believe what she was seeing, and panic filled each of her senses. Laying on the ground, inches from the still water, was a woman. Her light brown hair was still in a braid, though many strands had come loose. Her eyes were wide and bloodshot, and her mouth was stretched in a silent scream. Around her pale, graceful neck were deep purple bruises in the pattern of a rope.

Zoey sank to her knees and wept, her tears and screams soon drawing neighbors from their homes in slippers and robes. The gasps and cries of horror echoed through the park as they all realized Chloe Harper had been found.

CHAPTER EIGHT

7:42 a.m.

Less than an hour after Zoey had stumbled upon Chloe's lifeless body, Audrey had picked Vince up from the hospital and somberly driven to Lithia Park. They sedately climbed from the car and walked under the police tape to where Dr. Sheldon was working. The man hadn't gotten much sleep after the events of the night before.

Audrey rounded the corner of the trail and caught the first glimpse of Chloe's body, causing her steps to falter. As more light spilled over the bridge, the bruising along Chloe's fair neck stood out in stark contrast. Audrey felt her heart begin to race and the tears flooded her baby blues. Vince's breath caught in his throat as he stood behind her, and his strong arms reached out to support her before she collapsed.

Audrey threw herself into his arms, beating her fists into his chest in agony. Vince allowed her take out her rage on his body in silence, simply holding her close as she was wracked with emotions. He offered up his physical strength to her, knowing it was little solace in this moment.

The other officers and personnel on the scene quietly stepped away, giving Audrey her privacy as her grief poured out on Vince's shirt. The two stood like that for several moments, Audrey unable to compose herself in the light of such a devastating discovery. Finally, Audrey sniffed and swiped at her eyes before looking up into his concerned face.

"Drey, are you sure you want to be here?"

"I have to, Vince," she returned after a deep breath. "This is Chloe we're talking about. She was my best friend."

"I know, I know. But if this is too much, I can take over."

Audrey slowly walked to where Blake was writing notes and cleared her throat nervously. Blake's kindly blue eyes rose to meet hers with sympathy etched plainly in their depths. Colin Arthurs and his partner Angela stepped away from Denise to keep Audrey from getting any closer.

"Detective Stevens, I understand this woman was your friend, and as such we have to ask you to stay back," Colin stated with authority.

Audrey's vivid blue eyes locked with his own in shock. "All of the women we have found have been friends of mine, Detective Arthurs," she fired back. "Why are you shutting me out suddenly?"

"One," Blake said quietly, "because this is Chloe, and I know how close the two of you were. And two, because Denise just found something that might indicate you're in danger."

"Audrey's in danger most days, Blake," Vince countered. "What makes this any different?"

Denise came level with Angela, Sarah trailing behind her looking green. In an evidence bag was a crumpled piece of paper. Denise's long, dark fingers toyed with the bag in anticipation. This was the worst scene they had been to thus far with this killer, namely because of the victim, but this time the killer had left more than his signature calling card.

"He left a note for you, Audrey," said a somber Denise. "With the dice. He's not joking around."

"What the hell does it say, Denise?" Vince asked, anger streaking his tone.

"It says that Detective Stevens might wish to proceed with caution unless she wants to find herself victim number five," Colin answered. His eyes were on the ground as he dug the toe of his shoe in the leaves. His gaze flicked up through his impossibly thick black lashes and a frown marred his handsome face.

"Audrey, the killer is clearly singling you out because of your connection to the other victims. Now might be a good idea to lay low for a few days at home," Angela's voice piped. "I'm not saying we cut you out entirely, but it would probably be best for both you and Vince to remain offsite for the next week."

Walking up to the group, an exhausted Roger cleared his throat. "Are you guys done with the witness for now? Zoey was hoping to go home."

"Zoey? As in Zoey Bonnall?" Audrey asked, incredulous.

Roger nodded his head in affirmation. Audrey peered past him to see the young woman sitting on the bench twenty feet away, her head in her hands. She and Vince exchanged looks.

"I'll make you a deal, Colin. I'll head home and drop Vince off as well, but first, I want to talk to Zoey."

Colin and Angela shared glances and looked to Blake for assistance. He merely shrugged. Colin looked speculatively at Audrey before finally nodding.

"All right, that's fair enough. But no more than ten minutes, and then I want the two of you out of here."

Not waiting for him to finish, Audrey stalked over to a distraught Zoey, Vince on her heels. She hesitated for a moment then sat down beside her, gently placing her hand on her shoulder.

"Zoey, do you remember me?"

Zoey's hazel eyes slowly met Audrey's, tears streaming down her tanned face. Miserably she nodded. Vince squatted before them, puzzlement written in the depths of his dark eyes.

"You have the worst luck, Ms. Zoey," he commented. "Finding two bodies in less than a month..."

"Believe me, I know. One was more than enough," Zoey sighed.

"Should we be worried about your involvement..." Vince trailed, allowing the question to hang in the air like a heavy dew.

Stricken, Zoey's head shot up and bewilderment filled her eyes. "What? Oh God, no! I promise I didn't! I know there isn't much I could say to convince you of that, but I swear it's the truth!"

Both detectives sat silent for a few seconds, observing the distress plaguing her. Vince took her hand and smiled. "Okay, we believe you, Zoey. We just had to ask, circumstances being what they are."

Roger drew near once more and they gave him the all-clear to drive her home. True to their words, Audrey and Vince left the crime scene minutes later with a promise to join the others for a conference call at four in the afternoon.

Once the pair had departed, Colin and Angela scoured the park alongside Denise and Dr. Sheldon. The dice, having been found in Chloe's pocket, had already been bagged at the same time as the note. Denise had been busy taking photographs of the scene, finding what appeared to be faint drag marks in the dirt leading to where Chloe's body had been dumped.

When Blake went to turn Chloe over, he was shocked to find a single black rose lying on the ground beneath her. "Denise, you need to come see this."

Walking closer, Denise's breath hitched, and she quickly took pictures of the rose before placing it in its own bag. Colin and Angela looked on in interest, nothing about these murders making sense.

"Do you think the rose was left for Chloe, or someone else?" Angela asked.

"Well, she was a florist here in town, so maybe it had to do with that," Blake replied as he zipped up the black body bag. "I'll get her back to the morgue and get to work on the autopsy by later this evening.

I still have the man from the accident last night to work on first."

"Is he even a priority? I would think the autopsy of a serial killer's victim would take precedence," argued Colin.

"Under normal circumstances I would agree, but since the killer may have used the man to lure police to the east side of town so he could dump Chloe's body, I thought it might contain some important clues."

"Is that the assumption" Sarah asked.

Rubbing his chin in thought, Colin looked at his partner. "It makes sense. He would want to have as few witnesses to the dump as possible, and with half the departments focused on a major accident, this park was relatively easy to use."

"Damn, this guy thinks of everything, doesn't he?" Sarah groaned.

"Officer Lawson, I'm going to need you to bring David Harper down to the morgue in an hour or so for him to positively identify his wife," Blake informed her.

Nodding, Sarah strode toward her cruiser while Blake and his team loaded Chloe's remains into their van. Denise and the other detectives chatted for a few moments as they took a final look around the scene to verify they had gathered all the pertinent evidence before heading back to the station and lab.

—•—

8:34 a.m.

Vince walked into Ellsie's hospital room to find her staring out the window absently. A large white bandage covered her right arm from the cut she'd sustained, and despite the medications she'd been given, she looked like she hadn't gotten more than a few hours of sleep. He had a new-found respect for her integrity and intelligence, but also found himself fearful those characteristics would get her killed.

"Hey, Ellsie," he said softly.

Her head turned to face him, her red hair swishing around her shoulders in the process. Her big green eyes were full of sadness... not that he could blame her. Vince walked to where she sat and dropped down on the hard couch beside her, running his hand down his face in exhaustion.

"The doctor is saying you should be able to be discharged here in about half an hour. You ready to head back to my place?"

When she didn't answer right away, Vince turned to her with questions burning in his mind. Ellsie's chest was struggling to allow oxygen into her lungs as her tears threatened to overtake her. Without thinking, Vince simply pulled her into his arms and began slowly rubbing her back. The soothing motion had worked last night, and he was praying it would again.

"Calm down, baby. It's going to be okay. I'm not going to leave you again, I promise."

Slowly, Ellsie's tears ebbed and her breathing returned to normal. She stayed in his arms, comparing them to a haven from the evils of the world. Their bubble of serenity was burst with the arrival of the doctor coming to discharge her from the hospital, but thanks to Vince's efficiency, they were on their way home in minutes.

Ellsie frowned apologetically at the crumbs scattered on his doorstep and floor. "I guess I owe you a new bag of chips, huh?"

Vince chuckled. "I'm just glad you used them as you did. Although I do admit, I felt a bit like Hansel following your trail of crumbs."

Together they cleaned the floor and were about to head in for a nap when Ellsie's computer dinged impatiently. Both leery, they approached her laptop with obvious misgivings. Ellsie's sigh of relief to see it was a message from Sam checking in was heartfelt... but short-lived. Another email had been received only an hour ago. This one from the killer.

10:09 a.m.

In the stark, fluorescent light of the morgue, David Harper stood, chilled by the cold temperatures surrounding him. Nerves were on edge throughout his body as he waited for Dr. Sheldon to pull back the sheet shrouding the body on the steel table. From the blossoming in the stomach area, David already seemed to know it was Chloe.

That didn't make the image any easier to handle when Sheldon gently draped the sheet back to just under her chin, sparing David the sight of the livid bruises on her slender neck. David's fist surged to his mouth as her saw her, and tears filled his eyes. His stomach began to roil, a sure sign he was going to vomit. David dashed from the morgue into the hall and found a nearby trashcan to ease his nausea.

Sarah Lawson followed him out slowly, compassion written in her eyes. She allowed him a few moments to calm his stomach before they headed down the hall to speak with Detectives Arthurs and Guinabee.

***

4:00 p.m.

At promptly four in the afternoon, Vince and Ellsie, along with Audrey, joined their team via video call to discuss the cases. Vince and Ellsie were ashen, still shaken by the email they had found waiting like a viper on her laptop.

"The killer sent Ellsie a very disheartening email while she was being discharged from the hospital," he started. "More of his riddles, although this one seems to make sense."

Colin and Angela sat poised to take notes in the conference room at the station. Vince waited until they were all ready, then began reading from the email directly.

"He says, 'Ms. Lewis, I do apologize for your injuries last night and for my deception. I trust you will heal quickly under the watchful eyes of Detective Cortenza. It was necessary to keep you both occupied last night so I could have Lithia Park to myself. I'm certain by now you know why I wanted the focus on the east side of town, and despise me for my actions. Chloe's was a valid, necessary, and merciful death. Her husband would not have spared her had he been aware of her lies; I merely did him a favor. Chloe deserved something special, though; hence the rose. But one must remember that a flower deprived of oxygen will not long survive. Chloe's marriage was like a rose whose oxygen was slowly being choked; it was only a matter of time before it withered and died along with her. Give my best to the detectives on the case (including Detective Stevens, who I'm certain has not listened to my recommendation to use caution).'"

When he finished, no one said anything for several minutes. The only sounds were the pounding hearts inside them all. Sarah finally broke the tense silence, looking cautiously into the blue eyes of Chloe's best friend.

"Audrey, what do you suppose the killer means about Chloe's marriage?"

Audrey took a deep breath and looked at her hands

before answering. "What I'm about to tell you is not founded in fact, but more gossip. I have no proof of this at all, so take it with a grain of salt. We know that Kristy was supposedly planning to have a rendezvous with a married man the night she disappeared, and everyone suspected Elijah Middleton of flirting with Chloe. David and Chloe... they weren't the perfect couple everyone thought they were. David is a tad controlling, and Chloe was more of a free spirit. But they truly loved one another and managed to agree or compromise on most things."

Rubbing the back of her neck, Audrey looked into the camera with her anxiety hitting new highs. "Chloe had confided in me that she had done some flirting back with Elijah on more than one occasion, especially since she knew what a heartless shrew Bridget could be. Bridget is an ice queen and despises physical interaction with Elijah, which makes him more prone to looking for extramarital relationships. I know he's had a couple through the years and has somehow managed to keep them hidden from her. Chloe also mentioned how she was more than ready to try for a baby, but David kept putting on the brakes."

"How long was this conversation before she became pregnant?" Angela interjected.

"Six, maybe eight weeks."

"That's a pretty quick turnaround to get David on board with the idea of having a baby," Colin stated. "Did she say what changed his mind?"

"That's the thing," said Audrey, looking woefully uncomfortable. "He never really did. Chloe claimed that they had gotten drunk one night, him more than her, and had unprotected sex. David didn't even remember the night, but when Chloe told him she was pregnant, he just accepted that as fact."

"But you're thinking something else may have happened?" Vince asked.

"I hate to even consider the option that my best friend was cheating on her husband, but I know David didn't want kids. Chloe did, and Elijah did, too. With both of their spouses unwilling to consider the possibility of having children, they may have gravitated toward each other and one thing led to another."

"Dr. Sheldon, is it possible to run a DNA comparison on the baby to determine paternity?" Colin asked.

"Absolutely," Blake replied. "I can add that to my autopsy and send the samples to Denise. So long as you have David Harper's DNA on hand to run the comparison, it should only take a matter of hours to get the result."

"Okay, sounds good," Colin continued. "Moving on from the email and these clues from the killer, do we have any other leads to chase down?"

"Based on everything I went over the past few days, and now this development with Chloe, I would suggest we take a second look at Elijah and Bridget," Audrey declared. "Bridget isn't the type to get her hands dirty, but she definitely has money to burn on hiring someone to do it for her. If Elijah was part of her motive, that could explain two of the four, and all the victims belong to her book club."

"Good point, Drey," Vince chimed.

"As for the driver of the car last night," Blake started, reading from the file in front of him, "he had high residual levels of cocaine and heroin in his system. Clearly, he was a drug addict. I found close to thirty track marks all over his body, all at various stages of healing. Blood alcohol levels were surprisingly low considering you tend to find druggies often drink the hard stuff with their recreational drugs. I'm still waiting on the full toxicology report so I know the levels of drugs in his systems at the time of death."

"I can take Denise over to see David Harper and get a DNA sample," Sarah offered. "I can tell him it's to rule out any of his DNA on her body."

"Good thinking, rookie," Vince told her. "I guess let us know what you all find out, and Ellsie and I will keep you apprised if the killer reaches out again."

Colin shifted uneasily in his seat. "Well, there is one other thing we wanted to discuss."

Both Vince and Audrey looked on warily. Angela nodded at Colin, encouraging him to continue. Clearing his throat, he resumed. "We think it might be a good idea if we call up to Medford and ask for some extra officers to come down here to be a protective detail for you in particular, Audrey. The killer is making this personal against you now, and it would prudent to keep you as safe as possible."

"We already have a couple of your officers here who are helping with Vince and Ellsie," Angela stated, "but Ashland doesn't quite have the manpower to cover all of you."

Sighing, Audrey locked her eyes on the detective. "I appreciate the concern, but I have a state-of-the-art security system here and always sleep with my firearm on my bedside table. I am highly skilled at hand-to-hand combat as well. I think the protection might be more beneficial to Vince and some of the other book club members than to me."

"Audrey, with all due respect, the killer is targeting you as of this last victim. Doesn't that concern you at all?" Blake asked.

"Of course I'm concerned, Blake, but that doesn't mean I won't be careful. I have no intention of going places without taking precautions, so this is a moot point. The killer wouldn't be able to gain access to my home without tripping the alarm since only five people know the code. Even if he did bypass the system, he would still have to get past Declan and myself."

Grudgingly, the others finally agreed with Audrey and focused on assigning others to protect Vince and Ellsie. Plans were made to bring Elijah and Bridget in for more questions, this time with Colin and Angela taking point on the interrogations based on Audrey's suggestion. She volunteered to be present in the other room during the interviews in case she thought of something specific they should ask the couple.

With nothing left to discuss for the day, the call ended, and they scattered. Blake returned to the morgue to begin working on Chloe's body, Colin and Angela went to the IT department to see if they had had any luck with the emails Ellsie had received, and Sarah and Denise loaded up to go see David Harper. Everyone was staying busy trying to anticipate the killer's next move.

They knew the possibility of two more women ending up as victims was high, and yet still felt as though they were spinning their wheels on ice.

Saturday, October 19, 2019
3:38 p.m.

Denise sat before the computer and glared, almost as though she were willing it to work faster and give her results. Her impatience gave way to her waiting game, where she silently counted down random amounts of time to see if magically the results would appear at the end of her countdown. After nearly ten attempts, she sighed in frustration and rolled her chair to the other side of the lab, where her coffee rested.

"Slow?" Sarah asked as she entered the room.

Denise's violet eyes stared limpidly up at her. She was about to come up with a brilliantly witty retort when the computer chimed, sending them both scurrying over to read the report.

"Holy... oh dear God, this is bad," Denise murmured. "Very bad."

David Harper was apparently not the father of Chloe's child. Somehow the killer had known this and passed on the information to them cryptically. Denise could picture the look on both David and Audrey's faces when they learned the news. It was not going to be pretty.

"I guess the question is, who is the baby's father?" Sarah whispered.

"Yeah, and did David Harper really not know that he wasn't the baby daddy?"

Sarah looked shocked at Denise. The investigator was slumped in her chair, a mixture of concern and surprise painted on her delicate features. "You don't think David knew Chloe cheated and killed her, do you?"

"I've seen a lot in my time studying evidence, especially during my time in Montreal," Denise announced. "It's entirely possible he knew and planned some elaborate scheme to hide Chloe's death in the middle of all the others to throw us off guard. After all, there's no apparent connection or motive for him to kill any of the others."

"All that aside, Denise, do you really think David could have strangled his own wife?"

Denise sat in silent contemplation before answering. "I would like to think that he wouldn't, but I have to stay open and objective. Two things that this job has taught me is to expect the unexpected, and nine times out of ten, a murdered spouse points awfully hard at the other."

"The air seems awfully thick in here," piped a voice behind them. Both women turned to find Blake and Colin in the doorway. Denise nodded and the men entered the room, stopping to lean against the table.

"What's going on?" Colin asked.

"We just got the DNA comparison result on Chloe Harper's baby. David is definitely not the father," Denise informed them. Blake's face fell at the news.

"What's our next move, Detective Arthurs?" questioned Sarah, her voice shaky.

"Audrey suggested Elijah Middleton might be the father," Blake mused. "Is there any way you could get a warrant to take a sample of his DNA?"

Colin considered the evidence they had thus far and shook his head. "Currently, I can't really see a judge giving us one. If he wanted to offer it without one, that's one thing. But it might not be admissible in court."

"So, we're back to square one," Denise moped.

"Let me think about it for an hour or so," Blake prompted. "I'll call Audrey and see if she would have any brilliant ideas for convincing him to agree."

❖

"So, Chloe really did cheat on David?" Audrey cried once Blake had filled her in on the situation. She collapsed onto her couch in shock and ran her hand through her loose blonde hair.

"It appears so, Audrey. The DNA report was negative. Now we just need a way to get Elijah to offer up his DNA for comparison, and Colin doesn't think we could get a warrant just yet."

Audrey sighed heavily, closing her eyes to think the problem through. Colin was right, there wasn't enough probable cause to get a judge to issue the warrant, even with all the circumstantial evidence. And Elijah wasn't going to be dumb enough to simply agree to letting them take a sample without one.

"How about this, Blake," she began, "during the interview, get him a drink. Make sure Denise is on hand to collect the bottle or cup as soon as he leaves so we can run it that way. It won't be admissible in court, but we might could get a warrant if the DNA comparison is a match and search his home."

"It's not a great plan, but I suppose it should work for the time," Blake agreed. I'll pass this along to Colin. Thanks, Audrey."

<hr>

Sunday, October 20, 2019
9:48 a.m.

"Why are we back here?" Bridget's whiny voice snapped. "I thought we had concluded our discussion last week."

Elijah subtly rolled his eyes at his wife's dramatics. He looked nervously at his clasped hands on the table, the anxiety practically oozing from his seated form. Behind the one-way glass, Denise and Audrey looked on with blank stares, monitoring the entire encounter.

"Mr. and Mrs. Middleton, we just had a few extra questions we needed to cover with you now that Chloe Harper has been found," Colin stated from where he stood by the window. Angela took her seat at the table opposite them, a pen poised over her notepad.

"We have nothing to hide, detective, so feel free to—"

"Elijah! This is one of those times where you need to be quiet and just look pretty," Bridget hissed. "God knows you're not good for much else."

Elijah's face turned almost purple as she launched her insults at him, but Bridget paid no attention. Colin's brows raised in suspicion, and Angela nodded in silent agreement.

"Perhaps it would be better if we split this interview," he suggested. "Less stressful for everyone? Mr. Middleton, if you'd like to follow me to the other conference room we can chat."

Elijah looked uneasily at Bridget and started to rise from his chair. Her blood-red manicured nails latched onto his arm with surprising force. Bridget's almond-shaped eyes bore into his with a menacing look that would have withered a lesser man, and clearly meant to warn him to keep quiet. Elijah calmly removed her talons from his arm and followed Colin to the other room.

"Damn, that woman is a bitch," Denise chimed. "How the hell do you deal with her pretentious ass each week?"

"Some weeks it takes a whole hell of a lot of tequila to keep from kicking her Botox-ed ass into the Pacific," Audrey admitted.

In the room on the other side of them, Colin and Elijah seated themselves at the table in a relaxed fashion. Elijah expelled a deep breath and looked expectantly at Colin, concern plainly written on his face.

"I'm sorry, Mr. Middleton. I didn't even offer you a soda," Colin said calmly.

"Oh, well, I wouldn't say no to a bottle of water. If you're offering, that is."

"Sure, just give me a minute."

Sarah met him at the door seconds later, water bottle in hand. Elijah smiled at her before she dashed off again. The smile had not faded from his lips before Colin turned to him again. "Pretty, isn't she?"

Elijah blushed an unmanly shade of pink. Swallowing hard, he unscrewed the cap and took a long drink. Colin studied him, aware that the man was doing his best to control himself before he said something that would land him in a world of trouble.

"Mr. Middleton, we have reason to believe that Chloe Harper knew her killer," Colin began. "Moreover, we have received some unsettling information that Chloe Harper may have been having an affair, which could have provided motive for her husband to want her dead."

Elijah's blue eyes shot from the table in shock. *Bingo*, Audrey thought as she watched. Elijah ran a nervous hand through his styled brown hair and down his stubbled jaw.

"You seem quite shocked, Mr. Middleton," Colin practically taunted. "Do you happen to know anything about this information?"

"If I help you, do you promise you won't breathe a word of this to Bridget?"

"We'd certainly do our best, although if this goes to trial, there's a chance it would come out then."

"I guess it's better than nothing," Elijah sighed. "Chloe and I... I initiated the flirting when I would go into her shop. She was having a rough month and I offered to take her for coffee one day to talk. Turns out David was part of the problem. Chloe desperately wanted to be a mother and knew that the women in her family tended to have very complicated pregnancies. She wanted to get one over before it became too much for her body to handle. She told me David was refusing to even talk about having kids and it was starting to become a strain on their marriage. Chloe felt that he would change his mind about having a baby if she ended up pregnant, but he always seemed to keep his guard up about the subject."

"Sounds like she was becoming a little desperate."

Nodding, Elijah continued. "She was. I told her that I knew how she felt. I had always wanted to be a father, but Bridget... she loathes children. And she didn't bother to tell me that until after we were married and I brought it up. She laughed in my face and said it would never happen. I offered to step in for David if Chloe was still having a hard time convincing him."

"And did that offer lead to anything, Mr. Middleton?"

"Yes. Yes, it did," Elijah admitted. "Chloe and I met up at a hotel in Medford one afternoon and made love. Afterward, she didn't speak to me for nearly a month. The next thing I knew, she was telling everyone that she was pregnant, and that David was the father. He never disputed it, so I assumed it was the truth. Especially when she started having her assistant be the one to help me when I went to her shop."

Elijah slumped gloomily in his chair, looking defeated. Colin turned to face the window, a questioning glint in his eyes. Turning to Elijah once more, Colin cleared his throat. "Elijah, would you be willing to give us a sample of your DNA without a warrant demanding it?"

"I suppose so, but why..." Elijah's eyes went wide. "Are you saying David wasn't the father of the baby? That she was carrying my child and... and..." He buried his head in his hands, sobs wracking his muscular body.

Colin slipped around the table to lay a comforting hand on his shoulder. "We aren't certain of anything presently other than David was not the child's father. There is a chance it was yours."

"I'll give you anything you want, no warrant necessary. If that baby was mine, I'd like to make the arrangements for its burial," Elijah quietly told him.

Colin squeezed his shoulder and gestured with his head for Denise to slip into their room. Within moments, she had a DNA sample to compare with Chloe's child, and hurried to the lab to run the test.

1:18 p.m.

"Come on, come on, come on!" Denise spat, watching her computer. "The suspense is killing me here, you damn dinosaur!"

"Poor choice of words there, D," Audrey chimed from the door.

A blush painted Denise's mocha cheeks. "Sorry, Audrey. This whole damn case is really starting to take its toll, though."

Audrey carefully perched on one of the other rolling chairs and leaned back, closing her eyes. "No kidding. I will be more than ready for this whole ordeal to be over and done."

The two sat in companionable silence, waiting for the computer to finish running the test. Time seemed to drag on, stretching minutes into hours. Just when they were both contemplating running for a fresh cup of coffee, the computer dinged.

Denise pulled the report from the printer, still warm. Her violet eyes quickly scanned the report and her jaw dropped to the floor. Audrey raised her brows in question.

"You are never going to believe this," Denise gasped.

"Elijah Middleton would have been paying child support?"

"No... Elijah wasn't the father. Two up, two down, and no new suspects," Denise told her. "Now what?"

Monday, October 21, 2019
8:15 p.m.

The knock sounded on her door promptly, and Zoey jumped nervously from her couch to answer. The man who had called her earlier that day was from a news station in Portland. She had agreed to meet him this evening, although she was uneasy about meeting at her apartment.

Zoey greeted him warmly, thinking he looked familiar but couldn't quite place him. *Well, he is with a television station, so maybe I've seen him on it sometime,* she reasoned. She gestured to the chair before resuming her own seat.

"Thank you for agreeing to meet with me, Ms. Bonnall," the man said in a deep voice, pulling a notepad from his pocket.

"Of course, Mr. Hollis. So, you're with one of the news stations?"

"I'm actually a freelancer for a Portland paper, but close enough."

"What would you like to know?" she asked quietly.

"Straight to the point; I like it," he chuckled. "In all seriousness, though, you found two of the four bodies, correct?"

Zoey nodded. "Unfortunately, that is correct."

"What was that like for you?"

She shuddered. "Gut-wrenching... it was absolutely horrific. And knowing that there's a possibility of more victims being found is making me very uncomfortable."

He looked at her thoughtfully before setting down his notepad. He slowly slid onto the couch beside her and gently took her hand. "I'm very sorry you went through that, Zoey. Hopefully my next piece of news makes you feel better."

"Oh? What's that?" Zoey asked warily.

"You won't have to find the next body."

"Really? How can you even know that?"

"Because the next body will be yours," he whispered.

Before Zoey could react, the man's hand came down to the back of her neck, rendering her unconscious. Within moments, Zoey's body had been carried to the trunk of his car and she had been injected with a sedative to keep her asleep.

Zoey Bonnall was not part of the original plan, but her involvement required her death. *Wrong time and place, Zoey. Sorry,* he thought to himself as he slammed the lid and locked Zoey in the dark.

CHAPTER NINE

Tuesday, October 22, 2019
10:25 a.m.

Curled up in Vince's muscular arms, Ellsie was awakened by the sound of her computer pinging repeatedly. Apprehensively, she slipped from his embrace and padded softly to the living room. Tapping the enter key to bring up the screen, she shivered when she saw the numerous instant messages awaiting her.

"Vince," she called.

He quickly jumped from his bed and came to her side, his dark eyes narrowing to slits when he saw the menacing messages on her screen.

"Damn!" he breathed vehemently. "I was hoping this fucker would give you a break for a few days."

Ellsie rubbed her temples as she sank onto the couch. "Apparently not."

Together they read the messages, the taunting tidbits of information the killer deemed valuable to share with them. Vince wasted no time in grabbing his phone and grimly called Colin at the station.

"Colin, this sicko has apparently grabbed his fifth vic," Vince growled.

"What the hell are you talking about, Cortenza?"

Colin gasped. "All the book club ladies are accounted for as of two hours ago."

"He changed his victim profile on us this time around. He says he took Zoey Bonnall last night."

"That's the woman who found two of the bodies, correct?"

"Yep, she is." Vince closed his eyes and saw her terrified hazel eyes in his mind and could almost feel the fear she must be experiencing now. "We need to get someone over to her place ASAP to look for evidence."

"True," Colin replied. "I'll text Denise and see if she can meet us there. Do you want to come with me?"

Vince glanced at Ellsie's glazed green eyes and saw that she was nearly catatonic. This whole situation was going to break her. He reached out and gently took her hand, noticing with alarm that the action garnered no response from her.

"I should probably stay here, but I'll call Audrey and see if she can join you," he suggested.

"Sounds like a plan," Colin told him. "I'll talk you in a few hours."

Vince hung up and dialed Audrey's cell. It rang three times before she breathlessly answered.

"Hello?"

"You okay there, Drey? You sound out of breath."

"Yeah, I'm fine. Was just on my treadmill is all," she answered. "What's up?"

"The killer messaged Ellsie this morning saying he kidnapped Zoey Bonnall last night. Colin is grabbing

Denise and heading to Zoey's apartment to look for evidence. They were wondering if you wanted to go," Vince explained.

"He already took his next vic? Damn, this guy is on a roll, huh?" Audrey sighed heavily into the phone. "I've got to clean up a little and then I can head that way. Are you coming?"

"No, I'm going to stay with Ellsie."

"Aw, aren't you sweet?" she crooned. "All right, I'll talk to you later, then."

———◆———

11:45 a.m.

Audrey pulled up outside Zoey's apartment to find Denise and Colin already inside. She snapped her hair up in a ponytail and made her way inside as well. She paused in the doorway, allowing her eyes to survey the entire room before entering.

"Hey, Audrey," Denise greeted, noticing her slim frame. "See anything interesting yet?"

"I'm still looking. How long have you been here?"

"About five minutes," Colin answered as he reentered the living room.

Both wore latex gloves and booties on their shoes. Audrey grabbed a pair of each from the kit just inside the door and slipped them on, her vivid blue eyes still searching. There was a blank notepad still sitting on the coffee table, and that was about it.

"It doesn't even look like she struggled," she noted.

"You're right, Audrey," Colin stated.

"How did the killer even gain access to her?"

"I think I may have the answer to that," Denise piped up from the kitchen counter.

Both detectives turned toward her where she gestured to an agenda laying open. "Zoey made an appointment with someone from a paper in Portland to come interview her. He apparently wanted to meet here last night."

"So, you're saying the killer may be from Portland?" Colin asked.

"That's what this note in her calendar says. But I suppose it's entirely possible he lied to her in order to keep her suspicions at a minimum."

"That would make sense," Audrey agreed. "He's proven he's highly intelligent. Zoey found two of the bodies, so it would make sense for a reporter to want to interview her."

"Bag that, Denise, and we'll call up to Portland to verify," Colin instructed. "I'm not seeing anything else here out of order, do you?"

Audrey's keen eyes swept the living room once more, taking in each minute detail. Finally, she shook her head. "I don't see anything to indicate she struggled against her assailant, or any clue as to his identity. That planner may be our only lead."

Rubbing the back of his neck, Colin grimaced. "I was afraid you would say that. Damn. All right ladies, let's get out of here, then, and get back to work."

———•———

12:52 p.m.

In the dimly lit basement, Zoey Bonnall groggily came to on the dirt floor. Fear gripped her mind as she sat up quickly to survey her surroundings. Zoey found she was seeing stars as she moved, remnants from the blow she had sustained the night before and the drugs she had been given. She detected movement from the darkened corner and inched her way back.

"I was beginning to think you'd never wake up," a male voice purred from the darkness. "I was getting very impatient to play with you, Zoey."

"Leave me alone!" she screamed.

The heavily muscled man sauntered closer to her, his features slowly becoming more defined in the shadowy light. Dressed in black pants and a tight black t-shirt, he made a menacing sight as he towered over her cowering form. Roughly, he gripped her arms and hoisted her to her shaky feet.

"You know, I had very different plans for number five, Zoey, and you just had to get in my way."

Zoey shivered in his cold grasp and tears streamed down her face. With each passing second, she could feel more of the drugs losing their hold on her mind, her focus sharpening and instinct taking over. He had left the steel door of the room open; all she needed was a split second to escape.

"You're pretty enough, though," he whispered, his piercing eyes raking her quivering form. "There might still be some time to enjoy you before you have to die."

Panic raced through her as his words resonated within her mind. Summoning all the strength she could, Zoey reared back to kick him in the crotch. He caught her leg, spinning her body until she fell to her knees, ironically reversing their positions so that her back was now closer to the door. Trying again, she lunged upward to head-butt him in the gut, sending him into the stone wall behind him.

"You bitch!" he raged as his body collided with the wall.

Zoey turned to run through the door, but he recovered far quicker than she had imagined possible. "You wanna play, you little slut? Let's play!" came his threat as he launched himself at her, bringing her crashing to the hard floor.

As he tackled her, Zoey felt and heard her rib crack under the weight of his body, and the air abandoned her lungs. Her attacker flipped her over onto her back and gripped her throat savagely. Brutally, he pressed on her windpipe, leaving her even more light-headed than before.

When he released her neck, Zoey coughed and sputtered while he retrieved a length of thick rope. He quickly secured her, not noticing the small cut on his hand from the wall that dripped a single drop of blood on the bonds. As he tossed her into the corner of the dirty cell, the sound of quiet footsteps approached.

"Is there a problem in here?" a woman's voice chimed.

Zoey looked blearily past the man's shoulder to take in the profile of another person, one very familiar. Her hazel eyes widened in shock. "You!" she exclaimed, just before the man backhanded her and rendered her unconscious once more.

———•———

1:05 p.m.

"Excuse me, I'm looking for Detective Arthurs," a voice said quietly behind the precinct secretary.

She turned to find Elijah Middleton standing there, dark circles under his eyes and wearing a loose black sweatshirt and jeans. Her eyes filled with surprise upon seeing him looking so dejected. The soft click of heels signaled the arrival of another officer.

"Detective Arthurs isn't available presently," Angela announced. "Is there anything I can assist you with, Mr. Middleton?"

"I just came to see if there had been any news on the paternity test. I really just want to know if the baby was mine," he replied, running a hand through his disheveled brown hair.

"You want to know if what baby was yours, Elijah?"

Stunned, Elijah turned to find David standing in

the lobby only feet away. David's eyes were wary, and his countenance was one of exhaustion. Angela noticed Colin in the hall and motioned him closer in case there was an altercation.

"David, I... uh," Elijah stammered.

"What baby, Elijah?" David roared, his fists clenched at his sides. "Did you sleep with my wife?"

Elijah backed up into the desk, his face turning red with shame. David took a step closer, rage written in the depths of his eyes. Colin hurried to intercept him, keeping him back from his prey.

"David, please, I can explain," Elijah pleaded. "We both wanted a child, and neither of our spouses did, so we..."

"So, you decided to sleep with Chloe? You're lying! Chloe would never cheat on me!"

"Gentlemen, why don't we take this to a place a little more private," Colin suggested.

David shrugged Colin's restraining hands off his shoulders and stomped past Angela and Elijah to the interrogation rooms. The others followed in awkward silence, drawing the eyes of all in the precinct. Once the two men had been seated at the table, on either side of it to keep them apart, Colin cleared his throat to begin.

"So, obviously there is some explaining that must take place. David, the killer had been communicating to the reporter, Ellsie Lewis, that supposedly Chloe had been unfaithful. On a hunch, we chose to run a paternity test on the child your wife was carrying."

"Chloe had no reason to be unfaithful," glowered David. "I loved her, and there was a chance later that I would have chosen to actively try for a child, but we weren't ready. I only accepted it because it just happened."

"Unfortunately, the test showed that Chloe had in fact engaged in an affair, David," Angela stated gently. "I am so sorry, but the baby wasn't yours."

"That's not possible!" he screamed. "No!"

David threw his head into his arms and cried in pain. Elijah hung his head in shame. His blue eyes rose to meet Angela's, hoping she would give him an answer to his previous inquiry.

"Elijah admitted to having a brief affair with Chloe," Colin continued, "and offered his DNA for the test. We ran the comparison immediately."

"And? Was the baby mine?" Elijah asked.

"I'm afraid not, Mr. Middleton," Angela replied.

Both men's faces snapped up at her words. The realization slowly sank in that Chloe had been with at least one other man. David closed his eyes in despair as he began thinking that he didn't really know his wife at all.

"So, you're telling me," he breathed, "that not only is my wife dead, but she was apparently a slut as well?"

"Chloe wasn't a slut, David," Elijah reprimanded.

"She slept with me, you, and at least one other person, Elijah," David snapped. "You can't tell me she wasn't behaving like a whore."

"Do you even hear yourself right now? Chloe is dead, you asshole! It doesn't matter who she slept with, or who the baby's father was," yelled Elijah, his eyes aflame. "If you had been willing to give your wife what she so desperately craved in the first place, she never would have given anyone else the time of day."

David's eyes glowed with anger at his words. Colin rested his hands on his shoulders, keeping him from launching himself across the table at his employer.

"Trust me, David, Chloe loved you. But she hated that you didn't want to have a baby, and she also hated that she and I ever made love—"

Wresting out of Colin's grasp, David threw himself at Elijah, his fists connecting with the latter's stubbled jaw. Angela gasped and yanked open the door, calling for assistance. Roger rushed into the room and aided Colin in pulling David off Elijah's now bleeding face.

"Don't you ever say that again, you fucking ass! You don't get to say that you 'made love' to my wife! You're probably the reason she's dead now since the killer knew she cheated on me with you. You may as well have been the one to kill her!" David screamed.

"That's enough!" shouted Colin, as he pinned David against the wall. "It doesn't matter now! What does matter is finding out who killed your wife, Mr. Harper. Now, I suggest you go home before you get charged with assault. Roger, please see him out."

Colin shoved David toward the door and Roger escorted the enraged man out. Angela knelt beside Elijah, helping him to stop the bleeding caused by

David's fists. Elijah's eyes were filled with tears as he stared at the floor splattered with his own blood.

"He's right," he said softly. "I may as well have killed Chloe. All I wanted was to be a father. I never meant to hurt her."

<hr>

3:14 p.m.

"How the hell did the killer know that Chloe Harper had had an affair?" Denise asked.

"No clue," Colin answered. "From what we've been able to figure out, it seems she was extremely discreet about her rendezvous with Elijah. Even Detective Stevens, her best friend, didn't know for a fact the affair had taken place."

"What if..." Denise began before pausing to think it through again. "What if he knew because he had slept with Chloe as well?"

"That's an interesting thought, Denise," Blake commented.

"Especially since we now know that neither David Harper nor Elijah Middleton was the father of her baby," Colin interjected excitedly. "Denise, you'll brilliant!"

Angela sipped her coffee as she stared at her notes. Beside her, Blake did the same. Sarah walked in with a printout from Vince in her hands, interrupting Denise and Colin's conversation.

"Vince sent over the messages from the killer to Ellsie Lewis this morning," she announced. "It's ugly."

"Worse than before?" Colin groaned as she handed him the sheet.

"About the same, I guess, but this time he implies that he had intended to kill Audrey Stevens next."

Sarah plopped down in a seat as Colin began reading the messages aloud. The faces of everyone in the room went white, knowing one of their own was being targeted by a psychopath.

"Ms. Lewis, thought I would pass along a new headline for your story. 'Dice Killer grabs fifth victim!' I'm afraid I've had to deviate from my original plan of only targeting the ladies of the book club. Zoey Bonnall has simply stumbled upon too much of my plan, and she's going to have to be eliminated. Audrey Stevens, that divine detective, was meant to be number five. I had such special plans for Audrey... more than any of my previous girls. But alas, Zoey will have to do for now. I might consider adding a seventh victim and have Audrey take that honored place, but we shall have to wait and see, now won't we, Ellsie? Tell Vincent to call the precinct for you. I'm sure they'll want to search Zoey's apartment... not that they'll find anything, but they'll do it regardless. Have a wonderful day, Ellsie."

"Oh my God, he's truly sadistic," Denise whispered through the hand covering her mouth.

A commotion in the lobby drew all their eyes. "That's the chief!" Sarah cried. They all leapt from the seats to see what was going on. In the lobby, Shawn Mitchel stood staggering on clearly drunken legs, with tears running down his dark cheeks.

"I want to know who did it!" he yelled. "Who the fucking hell killed my wife?"

"Chief, take it easy there," Roger said calmly.

"Take it easy? There is no easy without Shannon! I can't live with this pain! I can't live without her!" As he spoke, Shawn became more and more agitated. His eyes were wild and bloodshot, his clothes wrinkled and stained.

From the pocket of his hoodie, Shawn withdrew his service pistol and cocked the hammer, placing the barrel by his temple. Shouts and cries from onlookers urged him to reconsider.

"Shawn, stop! This won't bring her back!" Blake stated. "I know it hurts like hell but killing yourself is not the answer! You know Shannon wouldn't want you to do this. Just put down the gun!"

Denise approached him cautiously, her lavender eyes filled with compassion as she got his attention. "Shawn...Shawn, look at me!" she demanded. "Look at me right now, okay?"

When his eyes finally met hers, a shudder ran through them both. "You are not alone with any of this. No matter how you feel," Denise told him.

"She's right," Blake agreed. "We are a family here in Ashland, and more importantly, we are your family. We will stand with you through all of this."

"I just want her back..." Shawn sobbed. He collapsed

in a heap on the linoleum floor, weeping like a child. The hand holding the gun faltered and raised, faltered and raised, before finally falling into his lap.

Colin gingerly stepped closer and removed the gun from Shawn's grip, putting the safety back on the weapon. Denise knelt before him and clasped his large hands within her own.

"I know you want her back, Shawn," she murmured. "We all do. Shannon meant the world to all of us. And you know we won't rest until we catch the person responsible for taking her from you."

The chief nodded his head miserably at her words, and Blake put a fatherly arm around the man's shoulders as he sobbed and waited with him until the ambulance arrived.Once Shawn was taken to the hospital, the officers in the precinct soberly got back to work. Colin and Angela returned the layout room they had been working in, Sarah trailing behind looking ashen.

"You okay, Lawson?" he asked.

She sank into her chair and slowly shook her head. Angela sat beside her and wrapped her arms around the young woman as she shook.

"That was your first near-suicide, wasn't it?" Colin asked.

Sarah nodded her head and pushed her dark curly hair behind her ears. Taking a deep breath, she attempted to steady herself so she could focus on the task at hand. Angela patted her on the back encouragingly, knowing a distraction was needed.

"Who do we look at next, Detective?" Sarah softly squeaked, looking at her notes.

"I really don't know," he sighed. "Angela?"

"We know the killer had intimate knowledge of each victim, and especially regarding Kristy Hillman and Chloe Harper," she began. "What if Denise was correct that the killer is possibly the father of Chloe's baby, and that was how he gathered his information?"

"But who does that leave us with for suspects?" Colin growled.

"Bridget Middleton has the most to gain and the most to lose in this whole situation. And her husband has admitted to the affair with Chloe. From what Stevens tells us, and what we've noticed during her interviews, Bridget is volatile. She would be a good person to take a harder look at, in my opinion," Angela mused.

"Are you suggesting Bridget Middleton may not be female?" came Sarah's shocked reply.

"I hadn't thought about that possibility before, but we can't rule it out. I was thinking perhaps she hired someone to get rid of her competition since Audrey mentioned she didn't like to get her hands dirty."

"Let's see if the judge would grant us a warrant to search the Middleton home," Colin suggested. "Lawson, will you go get Denise up to speed for us while we work on this?"

Nodding gratefully, Sarah hurried from the room, leaving the others to stack their papers beside the computer. As she walked to her car, she said a quick prayer, asking for help so they could close the case as soon as possible and bring closure to people like Shawn Mitchel.

———•———

5:18 p.m.

On a hunch thanks to Denise's idea, Ellsie sent an instant message to one of the killer's previous messages, asking if he and Chloe had had a relationship. She wasn't really expecting a reply, let alone one that would make any sense, but two minutes later her computer pinged.

Look at you, Ms. Lewis... starting to connect some dots, are we? I take it the lab determined neither David nor Elijah was the father of Chloe's child, so somehow you came to the conclusion I knew because I fucked her, too. I knew you were smart, Ellsie... although you banging Cortenza seems to contradict that assessment.

"Vince... you need to see this," she called.

He strode into the room and read the message over her shoulder. When he had finished, a string of curses in English and Italian spewed from his mouth, enough to make Ellsie blush as she rubbed the back of her neck. She was just about to try and calm him down when her computer beeped again, signaling the arrival of another message. Only this time, it was a sound clip.

With nervous fingers she turned up her volume and hit play, bracing herself for what was to come.

Squeaking sounds soon filled the apartment, the telltale noises of sex following. It was like listening to a sickening porno. Suddenly, a voice could be heard, clearly digitized to disguise the killer's identity.

"That's it, Chloe. Ah, fuck babe, I'm gonna get you filled up. David wouldn't do it and Elijah didn't get it done, but you can be damn sure I will."

"Oh my God, I think I'm going to be sick," Ellsie murmured, as the recording continued to play. Chloe's cries of ecstasy could still be heard, along with encouragement from whoever was being intimate with her, creating a staccato of emotions as she and Vince listened.

Fortunately, the recording ended after another few seconds, plunging the apartment into silence. The only sound was the pounding of their racing hearts as they sat, stunned by the dramatic turn of events. Apparently looking for praise for his tip, the killer messaged them a final time.

Enjoy the recording, Ms. Lewis? I bet it got Cortenza all riled up and ready to fuck you. We men are driven by the sounds of sex, and I know how he is with the ladies. Maybe when he's done with you, I can take a turn. I don't mind seconds, Ellsie. Keep that in mind when he takes you to bed. I'll be in touch, Red.

Vince bristled beside her as the blood drained from her face. Here was this psychotic killer threatening to sleep with her once Vince was done with her. Ellsie felt the bile churning in her stomach and rushed from the couch. She barely made it to the toilet before she vomited violently, her hands shaking as she gripped the sides of the porcelain bowl. The sounds from the recording and the taunting threat of the killer swirling in her mind was enough to cause her to continue to be sick.

When it finally seemed like her stomach had settled, she heard the water from the sink start briefly, and then felt a cool, damp towel being pressed to the back of her neck. Vince dropped onto the floor next to her and held the cloth to her forehead to cool her down.

"Thanks," she managed.

"Don't mention it."

They sat together in silence for several moments, waiting for Ellsie to feel somewhat better. She held the towel while they both had their eyes closed, leaning against the cabinets.

"I won't let him touch you, Ellsie," Vince stated quietly. "Never in a million years."

She leaned her head on his shoulder, her red hair swishing around her face. Gently gripping his hand with hers she nodded. "I know, Vince. I know."

⸺ ◆ ⸺

7:23 p.m.

Vince had called Colin at the precinct and updated him on the latest information the killer had decided to give them. He forwarded the sound clip and waited while the other detective listened to the disturbing exchange. He himself still felt almost violated for the threats the killer had made against Ellsie, and fear was in firm control of his head and his heart. His retrospection was interrupted when Colin breathed out heavily into the phone.

"Bloody hell, this is sick, Cortenza. I mean, we've come to expect sick from this bastard, but this takes the cake," Colin said. "How's the reporter doing after seeing and hearing this?"

"She's traumatized, as you would expect," Vince replied, glancing over at Ellsie's back. She had curled up on his bed with her phone and headphones to listen to music, hoping to calm her anxiety and keep from being sick once more.

"I can imagine. But at least she got us another clue."

"Yeah..."

"Have you contacted Stevens to see if she knows anything about this?"

Vince pinched the bridge of his nose and sighed. When he had called Audrey and told her that the killer was taking responsibility as the father of Chloe's baby, she had hit the roof.

"*What the hell do you mean he sent you a sound clip of them having sex?*" she practically screamed into the phone.

"*Ellsie point-blank asked him if the reason he knew Chloe's baby wasn't David's was because it was his,*" Vince stated solemnly. "*He confirmed the suspicion and then sent the clip, followed by a threat to take her to bed, too, once this was all over."*

"Great. Just fucking great," Audrey raged. "Apparently the guy is more twisted than we thought and now wants to go after the damn reporter on the case, too. Add to it that my best friend lied to my face, not once but twice, and I'm ready to crucify someone."

"I know this sucks but you've got to settle down if we're going to figure any of this out."

"I'll talk to you later, Vince," she said before hanging up.

"I did. It didn't go well," Vince admitted. "She was pissed that Chloe had lied to her and that we weren't any closer to figuring this shit out. Needless to say, Audrey is looking for blood."

"Sounds like our killer is, too. I'll send this on to the tech crew and see if they can make heads or tails of it for us. Although, chances are high it'll be the same as all the times before," Colin told him.

"Yeah... a dead end."

CHAPTER TEN

Wednesday, October 23, 2019
10:24 a.m.

The following morning, the detectives were no closer to obtaining a warrant for the Middleton home than the day before and had exhausted all possible leads for locating Zoey. A depressive air had settled over the entire precinct, a solemn attitude and expression on each face that passed in the halls. Time was running out; they all knew it, but there was nothing they could do to stop the clock.

Sarah swallowed a couple of aspirins with her lukewarm coffee and closed her eyes briefly to block out the harsh fluorescent lighting over her desk. They had all been working furiously and around the clock searching for any clue they could find to crack the case, and the long hours were starting to wear on her. As she rubbed her throbbing temples, all the phones in the precinct began chirping simultaneously.

Everyone grabbed their phones and looked in horror at the countdown that had just been texted to all of them. The seconds ticked by and Sarah's heart dropped to her stomach as she met the eyes of Colin and Angela across the room. They all knew without a doubt, the killer was telling them that in 25 hours and 35 minutes, Zoey would be dead.

* * *

Across town, Vince was punching the hanging bag in his second bedroom to let out his aggression after reading the text. Here he was, a seasoned detective who had trained to help others, unable to do a damn thing to stop this murdering son of a bitch from taking another life. He heard Ellsie's computer chime, signaling she had received an instant message, and ripped off the gloves protecting his hands to go and check on her.

Reaching his living room, he discovered she mercifully was still in the shower, the sound of the water running in the background a relief when he saw her screen. The killer had sent her a live feed of Zoey in what appeared to be the same basement where Chloe had been held, clad only in her black underwear, her wrists tied together and connected to a hook above her head. The hook suspended her a foot off the ground, leaving her completely vulnerable. There was no sound, but Zoey was clearly screaming at her captor as she hung there.

Vince squinted as he stared at the macabre scene, noticing a small stool was just out of reach of Zoey's foot, and resting on the flat top was a clock. The clock counted down just as the text message had done.

Sick son of a bitch! Vince thought. *He's tormenting*

her with a countdown of when she's going to die. What the hell is wrong with this fucker? He pulled his phone from his back pocket and dialed Audrey, his dark brown eyes riveted on the terrified face Zoey was making.

"Hello?"

"Declan?" Vince asked, surprised to hear the man answer her phone. "Where's Drey?"

"Hey, Vince. Audrey went to soak for a few minutes and try to think. I told her I'd watch her phone. Everything okay?"

Vince exhaled heavily and sank on the couch. "That depends. Did she get the same text as the rest of the precinct?"

"Why do you think she's in the bath? It stressed her out, made her feel inadequate, ya know. She needed to take a beat."

Declan's voice sounded off, like the case was starting to take its toll on him as well. *Well, why not? Audrey is living in this hell, and I'm sure she's taken it home to him. He's bound to be furious this prick is targeting her, too,* Vince realized. He closed his eyes in exhaustion and heard the shower snap off in the other room.

"Look, have her call me when she's got a minute, okay?" Vince told him. "I've got to go for now, though."

"Sure, Vince. Talk to you later."

Vince hung up the phone and walked to his bedroom. Ellsie exited the bathroom with a blue towel wrapped around her slender form, the ivory of her skin glistening with remaining beads of water, and her long red hair twisted and held by a clip. She raised a brow when she saw him standing there, the pain and anger burning in his eyes.

"What's going on?" she asked.

"Ellsie, I want to get you out of Ashland until this is over."

Crossing her arms over her chest, she studied him closely. "It's a little late for that, don't you think? I'm already a part of this... whether I like it or not."

He sat on the edge of his bed and reached over to pull her gently into his arms, losing himself in the soft silk of her rose-scented skin. Vince closed his eyes and leaned his forehead against her breasts, the heat from her body seeping through the towel to ignite his own. "Ellsie, this isn't a power play, I promise," he began quietly. "I really don't want you within one hundred miles of your computer at the moment."

Ellsie stiffened in his arms and unfolded her own so that they draped loosely over his shoulders. Her fingertips scorched his muscled back where they rested, and he lifted his dark gaze to stare painfully into her emerald eyes. "What happened while I was in the shower?" she whispered.

"You don't want to know, babe," Vince started. He trailed off when he saw her face harden and felt her nails begin to dig into his flesh.

"I'm not some fragile china doll! Tell me what the fuck happened, or I swear I will walk out of here," Ellsie yelled, her towel threatening to slip from her body as she spoke.

"He sent you a damn video of Zoey being taunted with a countdown clock of when she's going to die, Ellsie!" Vince roared, standing up to tower over her. As he had risen from the bed, her towel had finally given way, leaving her naked before him. He gripped her shoulders and gently shook her. "He also sent a countdown in a text to every cop in the precinct just before that. He's done hiding in the shadows with his threats, and he's out for blood. You don't need to be in Ashland until he's caught or killed!"

Ellsie shook, both from fear and anger at his words. She hadn't seen Vince get so emotional or vehement in the entire time she'd been with him. The rage burning in his dark brown eyes was like the fires of hell, and she feared she would be consumed by the flames if she stayed a moment longer. As she went to back away from him, he caught her arms and pulled her back into his powerful embrace, savagely claiming her lips with his own. His hands roughly scaled her arms until they tangled in her hair and kept her face tilted to meet his demanding mouth.

"I'm sorry, Ellsie," he said, his forehead resting against hers. "I didn't mean to yell at you, but... I can't let him hurt you again."

"Vince..." came her breathless whisper.

His hands were instantly on her waist, hoisting her into his arms where her legs wrapped around his muscled torso. Vince turned and laid her upon the bed, showering her neck and breasts with frantic kisses while his hands stroked her thighs. Rising from her quivering body, Vince quickly tugged off his pants and boxers before returning to lavish attention on Ellsie's ivory skin.

All the anger, fear, and uncertainty each of them felt was expelled as Vince skillfully pounded his body into hers and left them slick with sweat and tears streaming from Ellsie's eyes in the aftermath of their powerful orgasms. She clung to Vince's body, searching for strength to face another grueling day of this nightmare. As her heartbeat began returning to normal and her heavy breathing slowed, the sound of her cell phone ringing pricked her ears. Eyes wide, she fearfully looked at the caller ID and sighed in relief to see it was Alyce at the paper.

"Alyce, hi," she answered.

"Hey, love. Just checking in on you. Sam has her panties completely in a twist over this story, and everyone else is a nervous wreck worrying about you. We heard about the cops all receiving a countdown text, Ells. Are you okay?"

Ellsie closed her eyes briefly, wondering how to explain the past twenty-four hours to her colleague. "Honestly, no. It's ugly, Alyce. Very, very ugly." She pulled on one of Vince's t-shirts and slipped out of the room, holding up her hand to keep him in bed. She walked into the other bedroom and sat on the floor to continue their conversation.

"Alyce, don't mention any of this to Sam, but he sent me a recording last night of him and Chloe Harper having sex and claims he was the baby's father, then said he'd love to take me to bed once Vince is done with me. Then, I guess he sent me a live stream this morning of Zoey with a countdown so I can watch her wait for her impending death."

"Damn, Ells! Why the hell are you still in Ashland if this sicko is targeting you now, too?" Alyce cried. "Get out of here before you end up back in the hospital, or worse. None of us want to see you dead."

"I know, I know. But I feel responsible now. Like I have to see this through to the end, no matter the cost. And I know it's dangerous, but Vince watches me like a hawk, so I know he'd protect me."

"Ellsie," her friend softly reprimanded, "that's not the point, and you know it. Honey, this guy isn't playing. He's already killed four women, nearly ran you down with a car, toyed with you and the detectives on the case, has another woman lined up to die, and God only knows what else planned. You need to leave town."

"Did Vince ask you to call me?" Ellsie snapped.

"No, why?"

"Because he was telling me not one hour ago he wanted me to leave town, and now here you are, saying the exact same thing—"

"Maybe there's a reason for that. We care about you and want you to be safe. End of story."

"Look, I gotta go, Alyce. I'll talk to you later."

"Ellsie, wait—"

She hung up the phone and banged her head back against the wall in frustration. She wasn't one to run from a challenge, or from fear. Ellsie had to admit though that this whole ordeal was questioning her resolve. She hated being backed into a corner, and that's all she seemed to be lately. The door opened slowly, and Vince poked his head into the room, his brown hair still disheveled from their intimacy.

"Is it safe to enter the premises, Ms. Lewis?" he asked.

Ellsie nodded and managed a thin-lipped smile as he entered, his green boxers hugging his hips and making his tanned skin seem to shine like gold. He dropped on the floor in front of her and eyed her warily.

"I know this isn't a popular opinion at the moment, but I really do think it would be better if you weren't here right now."

"You're probably right, but what happens if this guy is never caught? He kills all these women and then just stops or skips town… then what? I can't live my life in fear and wondering if I could have done anything else to help catch him," she replied.

"And I can't live my life worrying that he's going to murder you."

His words were like a blow to the face. Her green eyes rose quickly to meet his darker ones, finding them full of tears and sincere grief. Slowly, she nodded, closing her eyes to allow the hot tears to splatter on the floor and down the front of the shirt she had borrowed. Vince gently enfolded her in his embrace, stroking her back with shaking hands. He brushed the hair behind her ear and cradled her face in his hand.

"When this is over, I will personally bring you home and we can decide where to go from there, okay?"

"Okay," she whispered.

He kissed the tip of her nose, then her lips, and trailed kisses down her neck once more before he carried her back to his bedroom to savor her body a final time.

———•———

Thursday, October 24, 2019
11:45 a.m.

Vince sat grimly at the laptop in front of him, waiting anxiously along with Colin, Angela, and Sarah as they watched the images on Ellsie's computer. He was grateful she wasn't here to see any of this, having gotten on a plane early yesterday afternoon to visit family in Denver. She had called him late last night to check in, reassuring him that she would call him every day to let him know she was fine.

She had left her laptop with him since the killer was communicating to them through it, and the heinous video hadn't stopped since it had appeared on the screen. Zoey was still suspended by the hook with the clock beside her ticking down. There were fifteen minutes remaining, and the tears were flowing even harder from Zoey's hazel eyes.

"God have mercy, this is sick," Denise stated behind them. "It's his own morbid reality show."

"Did you talk to Detective Stevens?" Sarah asked quietly, her eyes carefully avoiding the image on the screen.

"Yeah, Audrey is staying home," Vince answered. "Declan put his foot down, I guess, and pretty much forbade her from leaving the house until this guy is caught."

"Probably for the best," Colin said.

An instant message popped up on the screen, a menacing comment designed to let them know what was coming next.

A *dead witness tells no lies, Ms. Lewis. Zoey won't be telling anyone anything soon enough...*

As the time continued to tick down, they all watched in morbid anticipation as shadows shifted on the screen, announcing the arrival of another individual to the cell. There was still no sound, no indication of who the killer was as he was carefully out of view of the camera. Zoey was clearly pleading for her life as they watched, hearts in their throats.

The clock showed zero and three flashes partially blinded the camera as it relayed the scene. When the image resolved once more, Zoey's head hung against her chest as blood dripped down her body from the three bullet wounds. Her body swayed lightly on the hook from the impact of the shots and finally was still.

Sarah ran from the room, crying and trying her best to not vomit, as the others sat in stunned silence as the blood trickled to the dirt floor beneath Zoey's feet, creating a crimson puddle. Angela had her eyes closed and was muttering a prayer, Colin's face was set in a grim frown, and Vince was sketching the sign of the cross over his chest as the screen suddenly went black. A new message appeared, goading them.

I'll be in touch later, Red. Who knows, maybe I'll be generous and give you a clue on where Zoey will be found... and who might be last on my list. Tell Detective Cortenza hello for me; I'm sure he's around. I hope he's keeping you satisfied until I get my turn with you. Until later, Ms. Lewis...

"Son of a bitch!" Vince yelled, slamming his fists against the desktop. Colin laid a hand on his shoulder to try and calm him, but the other man shrugged him off.

"Vince! You have to stop and think!" Denise demanded. "Getting all riled won't do anyone any good, and besides, we've got a bigger problem to worry about now."

"Aside from worrying about who his next intended victim may be, we've got a daunting issue at hand," Angela began. "Zoey was shot, meaning the final victim will more than likely be buried alive if he sticks to the dice."

"How the hell do we find someone who's been buried alive?" Colin mused, rubbing his temples. "Oregon has millions of acres of forests, not including the regular land. Is he going to hide her in the woods, on his property? We don't know shit about his plans other than the next vic will be somewhere underground."

They stared at each other, waiting for inspiration to hit. Vince sank back into his chair and glared at the computer on the desk. "What we need is to know who the next victim will be so we can try to keep them under surveillance and hopefully stop this motherfucker before he grabs her. Then it's a moot point."

"But in the meantime, we should also be making plans with the assumption we don't get her identity in time," Colin continued. "I have a friend who works for the government. I can see if he can tap the satellites with ground penetrating radar to see if anything shows up."

"Good thinking, Colin," Angela commented.

Vince's cell phone rang, and he quickly walked into the layout room to talk in private.

"Hi, Drey."

"Vince, the countdown is over... do we know anything?"

"Yeah, Audrey, we do," he growled. "We know he's a sadistic freak who torments and then murders women for kicks. And in this case, he shot her live on the camera for us to watch. I'm just glad I got Ellsie out of town so he can't get his damn hands on her."

Audrey paused on the other end of the phone, listening to his ranting. Her voice was cool and detached when she replied. "He... he killed her on a live video feed?"

"Yep. And he's still sending Ellsie taunting messages about wanting to fuck her, too. God, Drey, I don't know what the hell to do at this point."

"But you just said you sent her out of town, right? Where is she? Portland?"

Vince sighed and sat on the edge of the table, his foot swinging back and forth like a pendulum. "No, she's in Denver. I wanted her to go to Timbuktu, but there weren't any flights there yesterday."

"Okay, then it sounds like the reporter is safe enough for now," Audrey reassured him. "Was it... was it horrible watching Zoey die?"

His breath hissed across the line, and he closed his eyes. The image of her lifeless body hanging in that cell, with blood running down the length of her, seemed to be etched into his mind by acid. "It was brutal, Drey. She was so scared and there wasn't a damn thing we could do to save her. This guy's running circles around us while we chase our fucking tails."

"God, I'm so sorry, Vince," she whispered. "Look, I know this is crap timing, but I wanted you to hear it from me first." Audrey paused and took a deep breath before continuing, "I'm leaving Ashland. Next week, in fact. I can't stay in the town knowing four of my friends have been murdered and I couldn't do anything to stop it. It'll just haunt me everywhere I go."

"Can't say I blame you, but I sure as hell will miss you. Why don't you come over tonight for a farewell drink, of sorts, and maybe you can take a final look at the evidence we have so far before you go."

"For you, I can do that. I'll see you at eight, okay."

He hung up the phone slowly, a feeling of heaviness weighing down his very soul. Not only had they failed to protect five different women from being brutally murdered, but now his partner of five years was leaving and the woman he was falling for was thousands of miles away for her own safety. Vince had never been one given to being depressed, but that was the very word to describe him at that moment.

<hr>

8:02 p.m.

"Where's Declan?" Vince asked as Audrey stepped into his apartment. "I figured he wouldn't let you out of his sight right now," he called from the kitchen.

"He had a big contract to finish, and since I was coming straight here, he assumed I would be okay," she answered as she tossed her jacket on the back of a chair. "I will be so glad when he gets done with this particular job. It has been hell on wheels with the number of contracts he's had to work on the past few weeks, in addition to everything going on with the case."

Vince reentered the living room with two open bottles of beer and handed one to Audrey, who took a long, appreciative drink. She looked around his place in curiosity, her blue eyes missing nothing. Arching a blonde brow at him, she smirked when she saw a pair of Ellsie's panties by the couch. Vince blushed and nudged them aside with the toe of his shoe.

"Look at you, player, getting all red in the face thinking about one girl," she teased. Eyeing the couch with obvious misgivings she backed up a couple steps. "Please tell me you didn't screw her on the couch, Cortenza."

"I've got more class than that, Drey," he said, rolling his eyes as he collapsed on one end.

"Keep telling yourself that, loverboy," Audrey countered, but sat down opposite her partner. "Have you heard from your little reporter since you made her leave?"

"Yeah, she's okay so far," Vince answered, taking another sip. "Talked to her about two hours ago actually."

Audrey laughed huskily, a mischievous look glinting in her eyes. "And were you in your room fucking a sock while you talked to her?" Seeing the look on his face, she added, "Wow. I'm impressed. Maybe change is possible for Vince 'Casanova' Cortenza."

"Grow up, Stevens," he fired back, kicking her leg.

"You first," Audrey said with a wink. "You know I love you like a brother, and that's why I tease you," she reminded him. "And let's be honest, I'm gonna miss you. You've been my partner for years. I trust you more than I trust any guy other than Declan, and believe it or not, I really think you're one of the good ones."

Vince looked at her over the rim of his bottle in silence. A small smile tugged at the corner of her mouth, and he found himself setting down his beer to pull her into a hug. "Thanks, Drey. And likewise."

Their moment was shattered by the sound of Ellsie's computer chirping from across the room. Jumping from the couch, they both ran to see what new nightmare awaited them.

Ms. Lewis... I do hope you haven't been ignoring my messages, but I suppose it's possible Detective Cortenza has forbidden you from using your computer after my comments about taking you to my bed. But here's a chance for you to solve some more of my clues.

For your 21st birthday and to celebrate your college graduation, you went out with some friends from back home. I decided the place you celebrated would make for a fitting resting place for Zoey. She'll be waiting for you where you had that crazy hot make out session with your boyfriend at the time.

As for your clue on my next intended victim, as the police call them, it's quite simple. I'm going to prove an ice queen can only be warmed up if you throw her in hell. Goodnight, Red.

"Oh my God, this guy doesn't know when to stop!" Vince growled when they finished reading. "I guess I need to call Ellsie back to see where this place is, huh?"

Audrey nodded, her face pensive as she stared at the glowing screen. Looking down at the bottle still in her hand, she quickly drained the remaining alcohol before she slammed it down on the table. "Got anything stronger, Vince?"

He chuckled. "Not tonight, no." Rubbing the back of his neck, Vince sighed in aggravation. Audrey walked over to the chair supporting her jacket and pulled the garment onto her athletic frame, Vince's dark eyes watching her curiously.

"I'll give you some privacy to call your reporter, and I'm going to go get smashed at home," she answered his unspoken query. "No sense in being here watching you tongue your phone while you talk to her, and I doubt very seriously we'd be able to find a body in the dark. I'll see you at the precinct tomorrow, assuming of course that Declan lets me leave."

She pulled her long blonde ponytail from the collar of her jacket and tossed him a quick wave before exiting his apartment. Vince watched from the balcony to be certain she made it safely to her car and had driven away, then returned to collapse upon the couch to call Ellsie in Denver. He frowned as her phone went unanswered for seven long rings, and worry gripped him when it went to her voicemail.

Why the hell isn't she answering her phone? he wondered. *I just talked to her a couple hours ago, and she said she was staying in all night. She should be right there with it.*

He hit redial and listened to the rings once more. Again, the call went to voicemail. Sweat broke out on Vince's forehead as he worried that somehow the killer had managed to find her anyway. That his grand scheme to send her away from Ashland to keep her safe had backfired. He ran his fingers through his thick brown hair, tousling it in the process, and wondered what his next move needed to be.

Hopping up off the couch, Vince sauntered over to her computer and dialed Colin, knowing he needed to apprise the other officers of the new tip. He took another slug from his beer bottle, grimacing at the aftertaste.

"Vince, everything okay?" Colin asked when he answered the call.

"Not even a little bit," Vince moaned. "The killer messaged Ellsie again with a tip on where Zoey's body will be found, along with a clue on who his final victim will be, but now I can't get Ellsie to answer her phone."

"Why do you need to talk to her so desperately? I thought the whole point of sending her out of town was to keep her out of this."

"It was, Colin," he replied, "but the killer somehow knew intimate knowledge about Ellsie and a celebration she had for a birthday several years ago. He says that's where Zoey will be found. I don't have the faintest idea where that might have been, so I need to talk with her."

Colin let out a low whistle. "Okay, I guess that makes sense, then. But who the hell would know that much about Ellsie?"

"Search me. All I know is sending her away didn't do a damn bit of good, apparently. This fucker is still fixating on her as well. I'm just glad she wasn't part of Audrey's book club."

"I think Mrs. Middleton would take offense to that last part, Vince," Colin chuckled. "I got the distinct impression that she ruled that club with an iron fist."

"Pretty sure Drey would corroborate that for you." Vince paused, looking back at the final message the killer had sent. "And based on his tips, I would wager the final victim is Madame President herself."

"What makes you say that?"

Vince sat at the table and focused hard on the computer screen. "Audrey is always complaining about what a cold-hearted bitch Bridget is. The killer says his final victim is an ice queen who needs to be warmed in hell. It makes sense."

"If that's the case, then maybe we can get ahead of this guy," Colin answered. "I'll get Lawson on it right away. Call me if you reach Ellsie."

The two hung up, leaving Vince alone again in his eerily quiet apartment. He eyed his phone again and finally decided to call Ellsie one more time. Again, her phone simply rang before going to voicemail. His heart in his throat, Vince left her a quick message.

"Hey, Ellsie, it's Vince. As soon as you get this message, I need you to call me. It's important. I—talk to you soon."

Hanging up, he tossed his phone at his couch, feeling insanely useless. *Who else would know where she celebrated her birthday?* he pondered. A lightbulb illuminated in his brain and he rushed to grab his phone from the cushions. Hurriedly, he dialed another number Ellsie had given him the week prior.

Anxiously pacing his living room, he waited for the call to be answered.

"Hello?" came a woman's voice, louder than usual to compensate for the ruckus of blasting music in the background.

"Alyce? It's Vince Cortenza," he answered.

"Oh. Hi, detective. Everything okay?"

"No, I need your help actually." He heard the volume weaken and assumed Alyce had walked outside to get away from the music. "I need to know about a certain location, and you're the only other person I could think of who might know it."

"Well, I'll help if I'm able," she told him. "What location are you needing info on?"

"Do you happen to know where Ellsie celebrated her twenty-first birthday and college graduation?"

A long paused came over the line, and for a moment, Vince was terrified she'd hung up. When her voice came through the phone once more, he felt his heart plummet. "Unfortunately, I don't. I do know she hates talking about that period in her life because she was dating an absolute tool at the time. Turns out the guy was married and hadn't told her. I guess he travelled a lot for work at the time, and basically led her on. She never would discuss what happened, but I got the feeling that they broke up right after her birthday."

"Did you say the guy was married?" he cried, warning bells going off all over his mind.

"I'm pretty sure he was, but you'd have to convince

Ells to tell you more," Alyce replied. "Sorry I can't be of more help, detective."

"Alyce, one more thing; you don't happen to know why she's not answering her phone, do you?"

Again, silence filled the phone with intense vibes. "She's not answering her phone?" Alyce asked slowly. "That doesn't make any sense. I talked to her earlier today and she told me she was staying at home tonight to decompress."

"She told me the same thing, and now I can't reach her," Vince stated, the worrying seeping into his tone. "This day just keeps getting worse and more confusing. Thanks for your help, Alyce."

"Anytime, detective. And please have her call me when you do get through to her."

Hanging up, Vince looked at the empty beer bottles on the table, wishing fervently he did have something stronger at the apartment to drink. Getting sloshed wouldn't help tonight, no matter how much he wished it would. Until he could get through to Ellsie, he would be spinning his wheels, though, and nothing would change that fact.

11:52 p.m.

The knock resounding on his door disrupted Vince's concentration. He had been scouring all of Ellsie's social media accounts for any clues regarding her past birthday, but so far had struck out. Glancing at the clock and seeing how late it was, he instinctively reached for his gun before walking slowly to the door. His brown eyes peeked through the peephole and were filled with shock at what he saw. He tucked his pistol in the back of his jeans and quickly unlocked the door.

"What the fuck are you doing back here?" he cried, pulling her through the doorway and into his arms. "Ellsie! Damn it all to hell! You were supposed to stay in Denver! No wonder I couldn't get you on the phone for hours!"

She wrapped her arms around his back and laid her cheek on his strong chest, savoring the spicy masculine scent he wore and the heat from his body warming her own. Vince reached around her and closed the door and then proceeded to back her against it, trapping her between his powerful arms. Ellsie's green eyes sparkled with unshed tears as she looked up into his face.

"Kinda hard to stay there when he's still texting me, telling me he planned to kill you if I didn't come back," she whispered sadly.

"So, you took a three-hour flight to come back to hell? Baby," he groaned, "I can take care of myself; it's you I'm worried about, though. He clearly knows way more about you than we thought."

"What do you mean?" Ellsie asked, fear lacing her voice.

"He knows about your twenty-first birthday..." he trailed.

CHAPTER ELEVEN

Ellsie's face went white. "H-how could he know any-thing about that?" she stammered. "I haven't talked to any of those friends in more than three years."

"What about your boyfriend?"

Her eyes narrowed to slits and she pushed out of his arms. Vince locked the door and turned to face her, crossing his arms over his chest while he waited for her to speak. After a few minutes of pacing, Ellsie sank onto the couch and hung her head in her hands.

"I felt very young when I met him," she began, "although I really wasn't since I was twenty at the time. He was going for his doctorate. He was older, more mature, fascinating... or so I thought. He quickly turned my head and I thought what we had was some-thing special. Turns out I was only fooling myself."

Vince sat down beside her and gently took her hand. Ellsie stared at the chipping nail polish on her fingers, unable to meet his intense gaze. "It was his idea to celebrate my twenty-first birthday the way we did. He talked all my friends into it, paid for the reservations, everything. I had no idea what to expect when he picked me up that afternoon."

She sighed heavily. "I should have known he was too good to be true and that a guy his age wouldn't be interested in me. Not really, anyway. He was always the perfect gentleman, though. He'd open doors for me, seemed to respect my boundaries, everything a girl hopes for in a guy. That night changed everything, though."

"Was he married?" Vince asked quietly.

"Yeah, but I didn't find that out until the end of the night. I never did find out what her name was, though. He had made sure that I went all out celebrating being legal to drink. Shots, cocktails, glasses of wine, you name it, I probably drank it that night. It was the first time he had pushed me to do something I wasn't convinced I should, but I gave in because he had always been so wonderful before. I thought I could trust him."

Ellsie let go of his hand and stood to pace the room again. Her red hair swished around her shoulders as she walked, and she rubbed her arms like she was cold. "We drove two hours up to the location and then spent the next three hours drinking. My friends had all gone to their rooms that, again, he had paid for, and he asked me on a moonlit stroll. I thought it was so romantic and sweet, and my dumbass drunk self couldn't see past his intentions."

She stood at the glass door leading to the balcony, looking out over the lights of the city. Vince could see her reflection, and saw the anguish written across her face. Her eyes were closed, lips pursed, and her breathing was ragged and shallow. He walked up behind her and gently wrapped his arms around her, placing a soft kiss on the top of her head.

"He took me down by the river, under the bridge, where it felt like we were the only two people in the world. It was dark and isolated. He'd convinced me to wear the sluttiest looking dress I had in my closet at the time, a little black minidress that barely covered my ass. He chose the perfect moment to seduce me. I was too drunk to think straight and gave in without protest when he picked me up and pushed my back against a pillar for the bridge. I hadn't even realized he had unzipped his pants and put on a condom until he was pushing my panties aside to fuck me."

She laughed without mirth. "And the sick part of it was that I enjoyed it. He knew exactly what to do to my body to get a response, and it felt damn amazing. Until his wife showed up."

"She actually caught you two having sex?" Vince asked.

"Yep," she replied, emphasizing the end of the word with a pop. "He knew she was coming. There's no way she would have found us unless he had told her his plan all along. She yelled at him, called me a slut, and promptly walked away. He followed her, and I never saw either of them again."

Vince stroked her arms and turned her to face him. When her face remained downcast, he hooked a finger under her chin and gently lifted her face to his. "I am so sorry that douchebag ever dared touch you the way he did, Ellsie. You didn't deserve that at all." He tenderly kissed her brow. "I have to ask three more questions, then I'll leave you alone. One, where did you go for the celebration; two, where did he take you exactly for his devious make out session plan; and three, what was the fucker's name?"

Ellsie sighed. "He took us to the Applegate River Lodge. If you walk down the path to the river heading to the bridge, there was a little side trail that led straight down to the water's edge. There was a pillar for the bridge there that he used. Since I was so drunk, that's probably the best description I can give you."

"And his name?" Vince urged when she paused for a moment.

"Dean Hollis."

Giving her another quick kiss, Vince released her and ran to his phone, dialing Colin as soon as he unlocked it. He relayed the information to him so that he, Angela, and Sarah could go to the lodge to search for Zoey's body. He would stay with Ellsie and try to find information regarding Dean Hollis in the meantime.

<hr>

Friday, October 25, 2019
1:48 a.m.

"Over here!" Colin shouted, shining his flashlight to signal the other officers with him.

At the base of the pillar for the bridge lay Zoey's bloody body, the ropes still binding her tanned arms behind her back. Denise, Angela, Sarah, and Henry rushed toward him, with Dr. Sheldon and others following close behind. Denise stopped in shock and Henry nearly ran into the back of her in the dark. The killer had jammed the dice into two of the bullet wounds in her torso, the sides with the gun and the word *morire* facing outward.

Denise and Henry quickly photographed the scene and wrapped clear tape over the wounds to seal the dice during transit. Blake was going to have yet another late night, as were they all. Carefully, they loaded Zoey's body into a bag and hoisted her onto a stretcher. With long faces and raw nerves, they all proceeded the forty-five minutes back to Ashland.

8:29 a.m.

"I think I've officially gone blind," Vince groaned, dropping his head on his arms.

He and Ellsie had been up all night scouring the Internet, DMV records, alumni lists, and anything else they could think of attempting to locate Dean Hollis. So far, they had found absolutely nothing related to the man she had dated years before. It was as though he hadn't actually existed.

"This is ridiculous!" she cried in frustration. "I dated the guy. How the hell can there not be any information relating to him?"

Vince's bleary brown eyes rose to meet hers and

his brow furrowed perplexedly. "You said last night he was going for his doctorate, but Alyce thought you two met because he travelled a lot for work. Maybe that's something?"

"He was studying for his doctorate, or at least that's what he told me, but yes, he was also travelling a lot for his job," Ellsie clarified. "He worked as some freelance software tech for a company up in Portland. I always saw him on campus and he usually had books with him, so I never questioned whether or not he really was a student."

"Okay, but maybe that's something. Could he have been a professor or assistant professor and lied so he could date you? We know he lied about being single, so it's conceivable he lied about his role at the college."

Ellsie took a sip of her coffee, grimacing as the bitter liquid hit her empty stomach. She looked into the dark depths of her mug and shook her head. "I'm fairly confident he wasn't a professor or anything, but it might make sense that he was lying about being a student. I just don't know where else to look for information on him."

Vince dropped his head back down, blocking out the morning light streaming in from the windows. When his phone began ringing, he didn't bother raising his head or looking at the caller ID but simply answered and put the phone to his ear.

"'lo?" he mumbled around his arm.

"Vince?" came Denise's voice. "Are you awake?"

"Unfortunately, yes. Been that way all night, too, D."

"You and me, both, along with half the department. Suck it up and listen," her strident voice resounded. "We may have lucked out with this one, but we could use another set of hands and eyes down here."

"Fine," Vince grumbled. "Give me thirty minutes to jump in the shower and try to wake up, okay?"

Without waiting for a reply, he hung up the phone and turned his head sideways on his arms so he could look sleepily at Ellsie. She offered him a tired smile and rubbed his back.

"Care to join me, babe?"

Ellsie chuckled, "You're bad. But yeah, I would..."

Thirty minutes later they were showered and dressed and heading down the stairs to his car together. He sure as hell wasn't taking any chances leaving her home alone after everything the killer had said about her. So, until the guy was caught, Ellsie was sticking with him. The drive over to the precinct was sobering, the knowledge that one more victim had had her life claimed by a psychotic killer was at the forefront of their minds.

When they arrived at the precinct, the electricity in the air was palpable. For everyone being drawn taut as violin strings, the place was buzzing. Colin flagged them down while he spoke on his cell phone, a brow raised when he saw Ellsie walking beside Vince. Beyond him, they could see Blake and Denise in the layout room with Angela and Sarah heading that direction with a tray of coffees.

"Okay, thanks," Colin said as he hung up. "Thanks for coming in Vince… and Ellsie."

She blushed the same color as her hair and stood quietly, waiting for Vince to speak.

"I wasn't about to leave her alone at my place a second time," he explained with a yawn. He glanced around the room. "Where's Drey?"

"We sent her to try to convince Bridget to come in to talk," Colin answered as they headed for the layout room.

"Good luck with that," Vince muttered.

"Mornin', Vince," Denise greeted. "Oh good, you're here, too, Ellsie. I wanted to run something by you real fast."

Her hands shuffled through some evidence bags, looking for the one in particular. She appeared to be unable to find it, so Sarah stepped over to offer a hand. "Which one are you looking for?"

"The planner from Zoey's apartment."

Without replying, Sarah walked to the other end of the table and pulled a plastic bag from a white box labeled *Case #298155-H*. Ellsie noticed Zoey's name written on the box as well, and the four other boxes around the room. Monica Simpson, *Case #298127-H*; Kristy Hillman, *Case #298135-H*; Shannon Mitchel, *Case #298141-H*; and Chloe Harper, *Case #298143-H*.

The sheer magnitude of crime scene photos and evidence bags, autopsy and toxicology reports was staggering.

Denise brought the bagged planner around to where Ellsie stood, showing her the page it was opened to. "We found this on Zoey's kitchen counter and noticed she had written an appointment in for the night she disappeared. It says she was meeting with a man named Hollis from a news station in Portland."

"Hollis was the last name of my boyfriend," Ellsie confirmed, looking green.

"That's what Vince said last night," Colin began. "Only problem is, we checked with the stations and the papers up in Portland, and no one has any personnel with that last name."

"So clearly he was using an alias," Vince agreed.

"Exactly. Now, for the dice," Angela stated, "they were crammed into the bullet holes, probably with the idea that they wouldn't be dislodged."

"What about the bullets themselves?" asked Vince.

"No bullets in any of the tracks," Blake piped up. "I can tell you they were 9mm bullets, but the killer went to the trouble of removing them."

Vince leaned against the chair beside which Ellsie had sat and hung his head in exhausted frustration. The others waited until he looked up again before they continued running down the latest evidence.

"I'm still waiting for the final analysis to be complete, but I'm fairly confident the drag marks are deeper this time than with the other victims," Denise said wearily. "But we did have a stroke of good luck with the rope."

Vince arched a brow and waited for her to continue, but Colin took the lead. "Denise found a drop of blood in the weave of the rope and was able to extract the DNA. When it came back male, she ran it against the DNA from the baby Chloe had been carrying and got a match."

"So, our theory was correct, as was that sickening sound bite he sent us. Our murderer was a daddy." Vince shook his head to dispel the notion that the same man had killed five women and somehow managed to father a child with one of his victims... and was still intent on taking Ellsie to his bed.

"Yep," said Denise, "gives a whole meaning to the term 'sperm donor,' huh?"

They all heard the approaching footsteps at the same time and turned to find Audrey joining them, a look of annoyance etched on her lovely face. Before they could speak to her, she held up a hand while she took a long drink from the coffee thermos in her hand, clearly needing the caffeine as much as the rest of them.

"Before you ask, no, it did not go well with Bridget," she stated. "She's such a high-class, high-strung lapdog who is incapable of thinking rationally."

"Take another few drinks of the coffee," Denise advised. "Your inner bitch is showing this morning."

Audrey flipped her off, which allowed for a brief moment of tense laughter to fill the room. They all sobered up quickly though when they looked back at the table to see the crime scene photos spread across its wooden top, much like a macabre collage. Audrey sighed heavily.

"I need some backup in dealing with Bridget, guys. She doesn't want to listen to a word I say, namely because she hates my freaking guts. She thinks I'm just trying to get something from her and won't budge, no matter how many times I tell her she's a potential target."

They all stared awkwardly at one another, unsure of who would be best to go to try to convince Bridget they were only looking out for her safety. Sarah opened her mouth to speak, but Audrey just shook her head.

"That's sweet of you to want to offer, Lawson, but that woman would swallow you whole then spit out your bones," Audrey stated colorfully. She gestured to the files in front of Denise. "Those the evidence reports from our latest vic?"

"Yeah, they are. We at least got full confirmation this time, though, that the killer was the father of Chloe's baby," she offered.

Audrey's eyes lit with surprise. "How the hell did that happen? And I thought the sick sound clip was confirmation?"

Blake shrugged. "Seems our killer dripped some blood on the ropes binding Zoey. Based on the clip, we ran the DNA and it came back a match to the baby."

"Well, there we go! Chalk one up to the good guys, finally," she replied. "Anything else useful?"

"Other than a circumstantial confirmation that the name of the reporter Zoey was supposed to be meeting matches the name of Ellsie's ex-boyfriend," Vince told her.

"Okay..." she trailed, looking hard at Ellsie. "Anything you might could offer up about him that would help?"

Ellsie shook her head miserably. "Vince and I looked through every database and website we could think of last night and couldn't find a damn thing. I burned all of his pictures from when we were together, so I don't even have one to show anyone."

"What about a basic description? Do we have access to the forensic artist right now?" Audrey pressed.

"Unfortunately, the artist is stuck in Portland," Colin told her. "Something to do with gang crimes, I think."

"As for his description, I don't think it'll help you too much since it could describe any number of men and he could have even been coloring his hair at the time," Ellsie answered. "But he was tall, somewhere over six foot, dark hair, blue eyes, perpetual five o'clock shadow, tanned..."

They all nodded around the room as her voice trailed. She was right; the description wouldn't be much help without the sketch artist working with her. Vince looked at Audrey and then Colin, a decision forming in his mind.

"All right, we've got to convince Bridget to put

her pride away and let us watch her. Angela, how did your interview with her go?"

"The killer got it right when he called her an 'ice queen' because damn, that woman is cold," she answered. She brushed her curling brown hair behind her ears, a slight blush painting her café au lait cheeks. "I don't think she'd listen to me, but I don't mind going to try to help convince her."

"Okay, then, let's get a move on," Colin stated with authority.

------- • -------

10:27 a.m.

"Audrey, I thought I told you to get your blonde ass off my property earlier," Bridget said, her arms crossed over her chest. "And why the hell are so many of your kind on my doorstep now?"

"'My kind'?" Audrey bristled. "I don't know what the hell your problem is with me, Bridget, but I've had beyond enough of your shit. If you want to be the next victim the dice killer goes after, he can have my blessing because I'm sick of trying to deal with you! Good luck, guys. I'm done trying to help this crazy bitch!"

Audrey turned on her heel, her blonde hair whipping around her face as she angrily strode off the porch and headed for her car. Vince winced as he heard the door being kicked before it was opened and slammed shut. He knew she had a temper, and he knew Bridget drove her batshit crazy with her pretentiousness, but thanks to this case, Audrey had an even shorter fuse than usual.

"If there's nothing else, then..." Bridget trailed, attempting to shut the door.

Vince and Colin both stepped forward and halted her attempt. She rolled her almond eyes at them and marched onto the porch, a look of contempt seared onto her face.

I guess her mother never taught her that her face would get stuck like that, Vince thought.

"Ma'am, we have credible intel suggesting you are the next intended victim the dice killer will grab," Colin began. "We think it would be in your best interest to allow the department to patrol and guard you and your husband until the killer is apprehended."

"Go watch that pathetic excuse of a man that I married then, officer," she sneered, her blood red nails digging into her arms. "I kicked Elijah out of here upon learning of his damn indiscretion with that little florist tramp."

"Chloe Harper is dead, and so is her unborn child," Sarah chimed.

"I don't give a damn about Chloe or her fucking bastard child!" Bridget screeched. "Elijah knew better than to fuck around behind my back, and now he's going to pay the price for thinking with his dick over his brain. Now, I do not need nor want your help, so get the hell off my porch before I take this matter up with the governor!"

Bridget stalked back inside her home and slammed the door in their faces, the sound of the lock clicking into place like the final stroke of a coffin being nailed shut. They all stood there dumbfounded, looking back and forth from the door to each other, uncertain of their next move. Beyond a shadow of a doubt, they all believed she was the woman the killer would grab next, but how to convince her she was in danger and needed their help was another matter altogether.

Vince jerked his head to indicate they should all retreat to their vehicles past the gate to talk. Ellsie leaned against his Ford, shaking from the screaming match that had just occurred. They all gathered in a circle to discuss their options.

"Holy shit, Stevens wasn't joking about that woman being hell on wheels," Colin murmured. "Threatening to call the governor on us for doing our damn jobs? I'm surprised anyone was in that book club of hers for more than a night with that attitude."

"Has she always been like this?" Angela questioned.

"Always," answered Vince. "She's been that impossible since the day I came to town and met her and Elijah for the first time. Bridget thinks she owns everyone and everything, so the local departments are too provincial for her. Hence the threat about the governor. Her damn stubbornness is going to get her killed."

"I say we get a patrol car to circle the block at least once an hour for the time being, and we can work our asses off trying to find this guy before he can make a move on her," came Colin's suggestion.

"What about Elijah? Do you think he needs any form of protection?"

"Maybe from Bridget, but I doubt the killer sees him as much of a threat. Besides, with the exception of the junkie used to lure everyone to one side of town, all the victims were women," Angela reminded him.

"I can stop by the bank and see if Mr. Middleton is there or at a hotel and see if he wants any form of safety protocol in place for him," Sarah offered.

Vince nodded wearily. "That sounds like the best plan we're going to be able to come up with for now. And so long as Bridget isn't a total moron, she might be safe enough inside that house of hers."

"I bet that's what Zoey thought, too," Colin stated. "All right, I'll call Anderson and get the patrol set up; Lawson, you go talk to Elijah Middleton. Angela and I will head back to the station to work some more with Blake and Denise."

"I'm going to take Ellsie back to my apartment and try to grab a couple hours of sleep and then she and I will get back to work on trying to track down her ex," Vince said as he opened the passenger door for her.

"Good luck to us all," Colin quipped.

Yeah, thought Vince, *we're gonna need it.*

Saturday, October 26, 2019
7:28 a.m.

Bridget walked with annoyance to answer her door. Someone was interrupting her yoga sessions, and whoever it was would pay for disturbing her calm. Knowing that Elijah had cheated on her numerous times through the years, but never being able to prove it, had been a bitch. Now thanks to slutty little Chloe letting him bend her over a mattress, Bridget was finally going to be able to get rid of him.

And that means I can run along down to Cancun and stay with Carlos, she thought with a smug smile. She had never wanted to marry Elijah, but their parents had said it was a necessary union to strengthen their families. She had raged against it because she hated how doting Elijah had been. Sure, he was attractive, but he lacked the sexual prowess and charm she had come to enjoy. The look on his face on their wedding night when he realized she wasn't going to fuck him had been priceless.

Finally reaching her front door, Bridget paused to push up her breasts and make sure she looked as sexy as possible... after all, a lady never knew when a tall, dark, and handsome stranger would show up at her door. Carlos wouldn't care one bit if she indulged herself until they could be together. And if he did, she would drop him faster than a fake designer handbag.

She opened her door and frowned at the person standing there in the early morning light. Placing her hands firmly on her hips and standing as straight as possible to make herself look more imposing, Bridget glared at her visitor.

"I thought I was quite clear yesterday that I didn't want your damn protection!" she growled. "What are you doing?" she asked as she was pushed back into her house suddenly with a backhanded slap to the face, causing blood to drip from her nose onto the cool tiled floor.

As the person standing in her foyer locked the door behind them, Bridget felt her blood run cold and realized she had made a terrible mistake. Eyes wide, she attempted to turn and run from the intruder in her home, but the other person grabbed hold of her ponytail and yanked her backward.

"Get the hell away from me!" she screamed, trying to claw at the person holding her hostage by her perfectly colored hair.

"What's the matter, Ice Queen? Can't take the heat?" came the sinister reply.

Bridget felt fireworks exploding on the side of her neck as a taser was used to render her unconscious. The pain was the last thought she had before sinking into blissful darkness. With Bridget incapacitated, the killer dragged her through the house to the garage. There, a hypodermic needle filled with a powerful sedative was injected into her arm, allowing the killer easily to pop Bridget's own trunk and shove her in, the now-empty syringe tossed carelessly aside.

Knowing that there were precious few minutes remaining before the patrol car went past again, the killer quickly opened the garage door and sped down the street.

8:02 a.m.

As Roger rounded the corner of the street in front of the Middleton house for the third time that morning, he was surprised to see the garage door open and Bridget's car missing. He pulled over his squad car and looked at his surroundings. There were no new cars anywhere on the block as far as he could see.

"Dispatch, this is unit twenty-two, over."

"Go ahead, twenty-two, over."

"I'm here outside the Middleton house. Last time I was through here the garage was closed. Now I'm here and the garage door is up and her car is missing, over."

"Roger that, unit twenty-two. Stand by for Detective Arthurs, over."

Roger waited anxiously for his orders, his eyes never leaving the expansive house behind the wrought iron fencing. He observed no lights or movement from inside, nothing that looked out of place aside from the now-empty garage. But he couldn't shake the feeling that something was off.

"Unit twenty-two, this is Detective Arthurs, over."

"Detective, how do you want me to proceed? Over."

"Backup is en route to your location now. Stay in your vehicle until they arrive, over."

"Roger that. And when they arrive? Over."

"Proceed to enter the premises, announcing yourselves, and keep your weapons drawn, over."

"Roger that. I'll keep you apprised, over."

He set down his radio and wait for the other units to arrive as directed. Within five minutes, two other squad cars were behind him, along with four additional officers. Together they walked carefully to the garage where they noticed the syringe tossed to the side. Morrigan Hammons called over her radio for a crime scene technician to be dispatched to their location immediately. She and another officer remained at the garage entrance, guarding the syringe and exit.

Roger and the remaining two officers quietly entered through the door into the mudroom, which had not been latched during the killer's hasty departure. Door pushed open wide, all three called out loudly, "Ashland Police Department!" Their calls were met with silence.

They continued through the home, noticing where Bridget had been doing yoga in the sunroom, her mat still laid out and waiting. In every room they entered, they swept the area to be certain it was safe, finding no one within the sprawling home. Finally arriving at the foyer, Roger was the one who noticed the drops of blood splattered across the tile, strands of hair pulled loose from Bridget's ponytail, and what appeared to be drag marks leading back the way they had come.

8:32 a.m.

Within half an hour of arriving at the scene and realizing things were amiss, every available crime scene tech and officer had been dispatched to the Middleton home. Colin and Angela stood on the porch with Denise, waiting while she dusted the door for prints. Evidence was collected from the porch, foyer, and garage, and one unsettling conclusion had been made: they were too late.

CHAPTER TWELVE

11:59 a.m.

When Colin brought Elijah in for questioning, the man was a complete mess. Apparently, being kicked out of one's own home and living at a motel will do that for some people. His dark brown hair looked like he hadn't bothered to pull a comb through it in nearly a week, his eyes were red and large, dark circles sat like puffy rainclouds underneath. Elijah Middleton looked, for lack of a better word, like shit.

He sank down and cradled the coffee cup in his hand, delivered by the charming Sarah. This time, his eyes didn't rake over her form or linger when she left the room. Instead, they stared, devoid of life, into the dark abyss of the swirling fluid in his cup. Colin studied the man for several minutes, not that Elijah was aware of the fact. Gone was the playboy attitude, the flirtatious mannerisms, the vitality he had exuded times before. He had become an empty shell.

"Elijah, I presume you understand why we brought you in today, right?" Colin asked. "Elijah? Mr. Middleton?"

"Huh?" Elijah finally replied, his intense focus disrupted. "I'm sorry, detective, what did you ask?"

"I said, do you know why we brought in?"

Elijah hung his head and sighed heavily. "Yes. Bridget is missing. I don't understand it, though..."

"Don't understand what?" Colin pondered.

"I... I know Bridget is a proud woman and can be ridiculously difficult, but why would she refuse police protection with her life on the line?"

Colin, along with the other officers in the adjoining room, observed his emotional state. This wasn't a man capable of deception at this point. He was broken, hollow, and upset. They were all surprised when Elijah began to sob silently.

"I know she wasn't in love with me, and honestly I don't think I ever loved her, either, but I never would have wanted this. She was still my wife."

The use of the past tense did not escape any of them as they listened to his bitter comments, but doubt still held them at bay. Elijah didn't seem to have a manipulative bone in his body. Least of all one capable of murdering five women in cold blood.

Sarah drove Mr. Middleton back to his motel, waving to Vince and Ellsie as they arrived at the precinct. Ellsie had the nagging feeling they were all missing something; her journalistic instincts were practically screaming at her. Unfortunately, they seemed to be doing so in a language she couldn't interpret. Reaching the bullpen, they found the others slumped at their desks in defeat.

"I take it he didn't have a clue, huh?" Vince asked rhetorically. They all shook their heads dismissively as he sat on the corner of a desk. "So, what's our next plan?"

"Well, Audrey officially gave her notice and is home packing, per Declan's insistence, so she's removed herself fully from the case," Sarah offered. Vince nodded and waited for someone else to continue.

Denise eyed Ellsie with her lavender eyes, a thought occurring to her. "Vince, the killer singled her out for a reason," she began. Noticing the question in his dark eyes, she gestured to the redhead seated beside him. "Ellsie, I mean. Not as a victim, per se, but for some other reason. Why else would he go to the trouble of sending her all the clues, the tapes, et cetera?"

"What are you getting at, D?" he asked.

"Why would he do that? Clearly, he knows her, and very possibly is her ex-boyfriend, but why risk telling her anything? Why include her in all of this?"

"Because he's sick fucker playing a game with us all," Vince growled.

"I think she might be on to something, though," Colin interrupted. "Ms. Lewis, how did you even become involved in the case to begin with?"

Ellsie thought back to the day Sam had entered office with the story. "My boss told me that the police had requested the best reporter she had to cover the story, and she felt that was me. Do you think that has anything to with this? I mean, Dean doesn't work at the paper, I can assure you. Sam doesn't even know his name."

"The police requested you?" Angela said, thinking out loud. "As in Chief Mitchel?"

"No! Absolutely not!" Vince hostilely said, rising from the desk. "Shawn has been one of my best friends for years, and I know how much he loved his wife. There is no way he had anything to do with these murders."

"Easy there, Cortenza," Angela soothed. "I highly doubt that he had anything to do with it, either, but we do have to look into everyone at the moment. Do you happen to know if he has any computer skills that would point in that direction?"

"I can answer that one for you," Denise chimed. "Trust me, Shawn Mitchel didn't know the first thing about computers. I can't tell you the number of times the computer techs were bringing up having to help him with various basic functions. He was strictly old school and hated technology with a passion."

"She's right," Vince agreed, running his hand down his face. "Shannon had to call me to come help them set up their media equipment at their house when they got married because he didn't have a clue."

"You helped them set up media equipment?" Colin asked.

"Well, yeah. I had originally thought about going into cybercrimes when I entered the police academy. I decided I couldn't handle dealing with the sick fuckers who terrorized kids by putting them in pornos though, so I switched to homicide," he answered with a shrug.

They all were silent a moment, thinking about who else would be on the suspect list, when Vince's head suddenly shot up, his eyes alight. Colin arched a brow, waiting for the other man to speak. Vince jumped up and paced briefly, his mind running nine-ty-to-nothing in thought.

"You guys are geniuses!" he exclaimed, excited for the first time in the entire case.

"How so?" Angela queried.

"One of the guys I was in the academy with, during my days in cybercrime training, he works for the FBI now in their cyber division. He's up in Portland, and I would bet he could help us."

Ellsie rubbed the back of her neck in confusion. The others in the room wore the same puzzled expression on their faces as well, but Vince was too wound up to notice. She lightly cleared her throat to gain his attention.

"Help with what exactly, Vince?"

"Huh? Oh, the video feed the killer sent! Chris is an expert in breaking down videos, images, sound clips, and more. He finds things that most people miss. He's got the best equipment in the industry to analyze this type of shit. I don't know why I didn't think of doing this before!"

"So, you want him to look at the video feed and... what?" asked Colin.

"Remember right before Zoey was shot, there was a shadow on the wall behind her, indicating the killer had entered the room? We never got any hint as to who he was because he stayed off camera, but Chris might be able to take the video, freeze it, and extrap-olate the killer's height."

They all considered the implications of what he was saying. The video might end up being the killer's downfall, even if he didn't appear on the screen himself. Colin's eyes lit up in memory, sparked by Vince's hypothesis.

"Another thing the killer may not have considered was the reflections," he began. They all looked dumbfounded. "Zoey's eyes were open, and presumably she was looking at the killer the entire time. He may not have stepped into the shot, but her eyes might be able to offer up the reflection of her killer."

"Damn," Vince groaned. "Why the hell didn't I think of that myself? I know all about reverse polarization and reflection uses. Yeah, so long as the killer wasn't wearing a mask or anything, Chris should be able to grab a reflection from either her eyes or the clock face that was there."

"I say get him on the phone and down here now," Angela advised. "We might just get lucky and find this bastard before Bridget Middleton finds herself underground... assuming she isn't already."

"I did call my friend about the satellites," Colin offered. "He's agreed to help us, and now that we know Bridget is missing, he's been setting up a task force to monitor the feeds until this is over."

"But that doesn't mean squat if he decides to bury her inside a house or other building, now does it?" Angela asked tiredly.

Colin shrugged. "I don't have a clue, but he promised he'd keep me up to date if they found anything.

In the meantime, seeing as how the killer has taken such a keen interest on Ms. Lewis here, and her relationship with you, Vince, I think it would be best if she stayed low, and so did you."

Ellsie's green eyes shifted uncomfortably. "How... how did he know that I was with Vince anyway?"

"I'm not sure that's the best can of worms to open, Ellsie," Vince warned.

"No, really. It's not like we were really seen in public together, and it all happened so quickly," she continued. "And like they said earlier, how could the killer have known I would be the assigned reporter?"

"At this point, it's all speculation," Colin surmised. "But I would say that your ex, this Dean Hollis, never lost track of you."

"And honey, Vince is legendary for his good looks, the ability to draw women to him in droves, and for being a fuckboy," Denise added. Seeing the annoyed expression on his face before Vince rolled his eyes, she chuckled. "Sorry for being the Queen of Obviousness, Vincent."

"You're hilarious, Denise," was his sarcastic reply. He held out his hand to Ellsie, who tremulously smiled before taking it. "I'm gonna get this one back to my apartment for now. Call me if you need me."

Together they walked toward the exit, Colin calling after him. "Don't forget to keep us in the loop on your computer friend." Vince waved in acknowledgement and left.

"Well... I've got to get back to the lab. I'm still running the killer's blood through the databases to see if I come up with anything," Denise told them, grabbing her bag. "I'll page you if I get anything."

"And now, we wait," Colin groaned.

Monday, October 28, 2019
10:19 a.m.

Sunday had been a complete bust. Other than arranging for Chris Thomassen to drive down from Portland first thing Monday morning, Vince and the others hadn't made much headway. Vince pulled his leather jacket off the hanger in the closet and across his broad shoulders. His eyes caught Ellsie watching him from across the room as he adjusted the collar.

"Where are you headed?" she asked softly.

Vince walked briskly to where she was curled on the bed and sat on the edge beside her. His long, tanned fingers gently stroked the hair back from her face and he offered her a smile. "I really wish I didn't, but I have to go to the precinct for a couple hours to help get Chris settled in to work his magic."

"Do you think I'll be okay here by myself?"

"The killer hasn't contacted us since taking Bridget, and while I don't like it, I think he's being quiet for a reason. He's gearing up for his grand finale, so maybe it means he doesn't have the time to screw with us," he answered. "That being said, so long as you stay inside this apartment and don't get on your computer, I think you should be okay, babe."

Ellsie nodded and forced a smile on her face. Vince, in turn, gave her his signature panty-dropping smile and a quick kiss before heading out the door. She heard the key turn in the lock and jumped from his bed to peer out the window. His engine purred to life and was soon tearing out of the parking lot and down the street. Biting her lip, knowing what she was considering doing was insanely risky, Ellsie shrugged on a button-up shirt over her tank top and leggings, and sat down at her laptop.

I'm so sorry, Vince, she thought sadly. *But I can't just sit here and do nothing...*

10:45 a.m.

"Cortenza, good to see you again, man!" came the exuberant greeting from Thomassen as he slapped his old friend on the back. "Although, one could have wished for better circumstances, but that's life for you."

"Chris, we can't thank you enough for coming down here to help us," Vince replied. "How was the drive down?"

"Not too bad. I listened to about half of an audiobook," Chris joked.

Chris grinned lopsidedly and shifted his weight as they stood in the bullpen. Vince and his computer genius friend could have easily passed as cousins with their tanned complexions, dark hair, and eyes, although Chris's eyes were magnified thanks to his glasses, and his hair was a mass of thick waves carefully tamed behind his ears. The two had been partners during one whole year at the academy and had remained good, albeit long-distance, friends through the years.

"You have everything you need?" Vince asked.

"Yep, I'm all set. That sweet little rookie, is helping get me set up in your layout room, and Denise is supposed to be joining me at some point as well," he answered with a wink.

Vince chuckled. Weeks ago, he would have probably gone after Sarah himself, but now he had Ellsie waiting for him at home. While her firecracker personality sometimes tried his patience, Vince knew he genuinely cared for her. And would do anything within his power to keep her out of this case for her own good.

Together, they walked into the layout room where Chris had all his high-tech equipment set up. Vince raised his dark brows in appreciation. *I had forgotten how much fun all these toys were to use.* Chris sat down at the central computer and began inputting commands to bring up various aspects of the heinous video where Zoey had been shot.

"Want to give it a whirl, Vince?" Chris asked jokingly, feeling his eyes studying the scene from behind him. "I seem to recall you being pretty damn good with this software."

"I'll let you sit in the captain's seat," he teased. He turned, seeing Denise coming their way, a grim look on her lovely face. "Denise, you look beyond tense."

"Morning to you, too, Vince," she said as she entered the room. "And tense is an understatement. We were going over the car that tried to run down your reporter girl the night Chloe was dumped and found something caught in the wreckage we hadn't seen before."

Brow furrowing, Vince crossed his arms over his muscled chest as he remembered the scene. The look of terror on Ellsie's face as the car had barreled toward her, intent on ending her life in that stinking alley. The sound of the metal slamming into the wall with an unforgiving force, crumpling the car like an aluminum can.

"It's a wonder you were able to find anything in that piece of shit."

"Yeah, well you're going to be pissed when you see this," she said, holding out an evidence bag to him.

Inside was a wrinkled and partially torn pair of photographs. They had clearly been taken outside of Vince's apartment, and while one showed him and Ellsie in a passionate embrace, the other was only of her, clad in her bra and panties, smiling.

"What the actual fuck?" he roared, a slew of Italian curse words following.

Chris and Denise eyed him with worry. He tossed

the photos back at Denise to catch and whipped out his cell phone. Dialing Ellsie, he waited for her to answer.

"Damn it, damn it, damn it! Why the hell isn't she answering?"

"Go check on her, Vince," Chris told him levelly, "Denise and I will stay here and keep working."

———•———

11:22 a.m.

I think I've got everything, Ellsie thought as she played with her ponytail. She was about to unlock the door when it burst open, an anxious Vince rushing through. Eyes wide, Ellsie back up quickly, realizing her plans just got tanked.

"Why the hell didn't you pick up when I called?" he asked, reaching for her.

Behind her, the computer pinged, drawing his attention and his dark, wrathful gaze. "Ellsie... what the fuck did you do?"

She bit her lip and looked at the floor, her heart pounding in her chest. Vince's dark eyes radiated anger as he forced her to back up until they were level with the table holding her computer. Thinking perhaps she could run past him, she made a motion to take off, only to have Vince's powerful arms hold her in place.

I'm surprised at you, Ellsie, wanting to see me

again. I didn't think that would go over so well with your new lover. And you're worth twenty of Bridget Middleton, so I'd be pretty foolish to reject you taking her place. Maybe this time my wife can join us, huh? See you soon, Red.

"You... you contacted that son of a bitch and offered to trade places with Bridget?" came his faltering voice. "Why? Why would you do that, babe?"

"It's Dean, Vince. I know how crazy it seems, but I'm sure he wouldn't kill me and—"

"Have you lost your fucking mind?" he exploded. "He's a damn murderer, Ellsie, not someone to mess with! And you thought you could what? Convince him to turn himself in? Get a fucking grip! He would just as easily slit your throat because of what you know about him."

"I couldn't just sit here! I had to do something, Vince! There's a reason he involved me in this, and I don't think it was to kill me."

He towered over her and glared into her defiant green eyes. "Oh, really? You really don't have a clue, Ellsie. Some great investigative journalist you are. He gave a picture of you in practically nothing to the junkie who tried to run you down that night. Whether you were to be payment for drugs or what, I don't know, but he fully intended for you to die that night."

Anger lit in her eyes as he berated her, and she began to struggle against his powerful hold. "Let me go, you bastard!"

"Right... I'm the bastard because I want to keep you alive and not let you become another victim of this sick fucker, but he's a saint despite practically raping you and murdering five women and an unborn child. His child, might I remind you," Vince growled.

"Let. Me. Go."

"Oh, I don't think so, Ellsie. I'm going to make sure you don't do anything like this again, baby."

At his tone, fear pricked in her mind. She looked up to see his usually warm brown eyes filled with rage, with malice. And before she could scream, his hand came down in a chopping motion on the side of her neck, sending her into the oblivion of darkness.

⸻ • ⸻

4:07 p.m.

"Hey man, how are you holding up?"

"I've been better, Vince, you?"

"Shit, I can imagine, Shawn. Been dealing with my own set of drama today, honestly," Vince told his boss as he sat on the couch beside him. "Hopefully I don't hit a nerve with this, but it seems so fucking weird to be sitting here without Shannon in that insanely bright kitchen of hers."

Shawn nodded miserably. "Yeah, I've been thinking that pretty much every moment I'm awake here lately. And thanks for coming over, by the way."

"Anytime. I'm here for you; I hope you know that," Vince answered. "The whole department is."

Shawn sighed and looked down at his wedding band again. "I know. And honestly, I almost needed to talk to Audrey, too, but she's so busy with packing, and she said it would be too emotional right now to talk about Shannon."

Vince nodded, still not following the other man's disjointed thought processes. When Shawn had called him an hour earlier, asking him to come over for a beer and to talk about Shannon, Vince had initially been hesitant. Between the mess with Ellsie at his place he'd had to clean up and everything else, he wasn't sure this was the best idea. But Shawn had been insistent, and he couldn't turn the man down no matter how hard he tried.

"What's on your mind, Shawn," he asked, cutting to the chase at last.

"I was just trying to make sense of Shannon's last days here on earth. Audrey had met with her right before it happened, so I had hoped she could shed some more light on the subject, but..."

"She's too emotional, like you said," Vince finished. "And yeah, I remember Audrey taking a break to go meet her for coffee. It was right after we had found Kristy's body."

"Shannon had been so upset that evening when I got home. I guess she had told Audrey what happened at Chloe's shop, and Audrey blew up at her."

Vince eyed the other man speculatively. When

Audrey had returned from that coffee date, she had said something to the effect of a misunderstanding someone had told her and Shannon. Was Shannon referring to something else when talking about it to Shawn?

"What did she see at Chloe's shop?"

Shawn nervously rubbed the back of his neck, an almost sheepish expression on his face. "I guess she had been in the shop looking for some flowers for a friend and had seen Declan flirting with Chloe. When she told Audrey about it, she didn't take it very well. I guess Audrey accused her of trying to start a rumor to make her look bad and she didn't appreciate it. Shannon was really hurt over the whole exchange."

"Wait a second!" Vince said, holding up his hands. "Shannon is the one who told Audrey about Declan's so-called flirting?" *And with Chloe, no less.*

"Yeah, why?"

"Shawn, I've got to go for now, but you may have just given me an idea."

Shawn watched in surprise as Vince jumped from the couch and jogged out the door, his engine roaring to life seconds later.

⬥

4:52 p.m.

"Sarah!" Vince yelled, startling the young officer as she sat at her desk.

He was running at full speed until he stopped by

her side, a look of panic on his handsome face. His shouting had drawn the attention of Colin, Denise, and Chris, who all approached quickly.

"Yes, detective?" Sarah answered.

"Do you remember the day that Audrey went to have coffee with Shannon?"

"Um, I think so."

"Okay, what did she say about the coffee date?" he asked, throwing his jacket onto the chair.

Sarah scratched her head briefly, trying to conjure the conversation from that day to the forefront of her mind. "She said she was late coming back because there was a misunderstanding that needed to be addressed because someone had told her and Shannon that Declan had been flirting with another woman."

"Good, I'm glad you remembered the exact same thing I did," he confirmed, pulling out a file with the computer print outs of the killer's messages. "But I was just with Shawn, who is telling a different story, and it got me thinking..."

"What was different about his story from the one Audrey told you?" Denise asked in surprise.

"He said Shannon had come home upset because Audrey had gotten mad at her for telling Audrey that Declan was flirting... with Chloe Harper of all people," Vince answered. Finally finding the page he was looking for, he slammed it on the desk. "Here, look at this."

"The clues from the killer on why he killed each victim?" Colin pondered, stepping closer.

"Yeah, look at the one for Shannon again," Vince encouraged.

"'Rumors are like poison... share them at your own risk...'" Colin read aloud. "Shannon was poisoned, and brutally. And now, according to Shawn, she was the one sharing what could be considered a rumor, I suppose."

"Oh, God," Denise breathed. "Are you suggesting what I think you are?"

"I'm saying it's possible that Declan Stevens had an affair with Chloe... and with Shannon sharing that information with Audrey, maybe he felt threatened," came Vince's stoic reply.

"And if he is the killer, feeling threatened might have caused him to feel the need to silence both Shannon and Chloe," Colin mused. "It actually makes sense."

"Yeah, but how could he get away with murdering five women and Detective Stevens not knowing any-thing about it?" Sarah asked, her eyes wide.

"You just took the words right out of my mouth, Sarah," Denise chirped. "Come on, Vince. You and I both know Audrey would've figured something like that out if it were him. He's too mellow of a guy to be a killer."

"Face it, Denise, none of us really know Declan all that well," he countered. "In the five years I've been her partner, I've never been in their house, but I do know they have close to ten acres and several work-shops on the property. She's a workaholic, and he does freelance—"

"Vince?" Colin spoke his name when the other man suddenly cut off his sentence halfway through a thought. "What did you think of?"

"He does freelance..." Vince breathed. "He travels a lot, for various clients, a lot of whom are in Northern California."

"Northern California is where Ellsie went to college, right?" Sarah asked.

"Yeah. And Declan is always on his computer from what Audrey says."

"Are we seriously considering that one of our best officer's spouses is capable of masterminding six brutal murders and keeping it from her?" Denise asked once more. "Look, I know Declan is a bit of a recluse and hardly ever shows up in town, but that doesn't make him guilty of murder, guys."

"No, but I have an idea," Vince told her, tapping quickly on his phone while walking down the hall. Colin and Denise both shrugged and followed him toward the rear of the building.

Vince entered a room at the back that led to their four holding cells, his phone in his pocket now. He walked to the cell at the far end of the room, meeting the furious eyes of the person within the bars.

"Unless you've come to let me out of this fucking cell, Vince, I suggest you turn around and leave," Ellsie snapped.

Her green eyes blazed as he drew nearer, her neck still sore from where he had struck her. When she had finally come to, she had found herself locked in the cell, Vince sitting in a folding chair just outside the bars.

"What the hell, Vince?"

"I told you, I had to make sure you didn't end up getting yourself killed," he had answered solemnly. "This was the only thing I could think of because, let's face it, I sent you hours away to Denver and you came running back when that bastard texted you. God only knows what you would have done had I not stopped you from leaving my apartment."

"Go to hell, Cortenza!"

"All right, fine. I'll go to hell, Ellsie. But it sure won't be for allowing you to be his next victim."

He had risen at that point and taken his chair back to the desk at the far end of the room, throwing her a little wave before exiting the room and leaving her to deal with her rage alone.

"I'll leave in a minute, Ellsie. First, I need you to look at this picture and tell me if you know him." He pulled his phone from his pocket and flipped the switch to turn it back on. He held it up, but she had turned her back to him.

"Why the hell would I help you after you locked me in here?"

"I did it to save your fucking life!" he hissed. "If you don't care if you die, fine, I'll let you run straight into the arms of a murderer. But I still happen to care about you, so damn it, let me keep you safe! Now look at the fucking picture!"

"Fine!" she snapped, turning around to look at

him. "I'll look at it, but I still don't—what the hell?" She stiffened in shock as she looked at the screen. "How did you find his picture? We've been looking for days and couldn't find it anywhere."

"Is this Dean?"

"Yeah, that's him. I don't understand... Vince? Why the hell do you look like you're gonna puke?"

"His name isn't Dean Hollis, Ellsie. It's Declan Stevens..."

CHAPTER THIRTEEN

"Declan Stevens?" she squeaked. "As in, Detective Stevens's husband, Declan Stevens?"

Vince curled a hand around the bars of her cell and lightly banged his forehead against the cool metal poles. Denise and Colin eased into the room, looks of pure shock plastered on their faces. Thoughts were swirling through their minds like a raging vortex of terror, threatening to destroy everyone in its path.

"He… he killed seven people and tried to kill two more," Denise whispered. "How did we miss this?"

"I don't care how we missed it, but we sure as hell are going to finish it," Vince growled. "Let's get our shit together and go arrest this sick fucker."

"Hey, Vince!" came a yell from the other room.

"Colin, let her out," Vince said, gesturing to Ellsie before turning his dark gaze on her, "so long as she promises to stay here and not do anything stupid."

Turning on his heel before she could respond, Vince strode quickly back into the bullpen and headed for the layout room, where Chris was wait-ing. A stilled image from the video was on the screen, measurement markers along the length of the shadow and Zoey's body.

"So, I tried to reverse the polarity to give us a reflection from Zoey's eyes or the clock, hoping to get an image of this guy, but it didn't work. There were too many opposing factors, making it impossible," the tech started.

"I knew it was a long shot, but damn, I was hoping you would get lucky."

"Vince, we've got a problem, man," Chris told him slowly.

"Yeah, it's called a fucking serial killer named Declan," Vince snapped grouchily.

"And how tall is this guy?"

"He's like... six feet, four or five inches, I think," he answered. "He's about the same height as me." He noticed the look on Chris's face. "Why?"

"Then he's not your killer," Chris said. "At least not for Zoey Bonnall."

Jaws hitting the floor in unison, Vince, Denise, and Sarah all looked at the screen once more. "What the hell are you saying, Thomassen?" Vince's jaw locked firmly into place, dark brows furrowed, and an aura of extreme tension ebbed around his muscled form.

"According to these measurements, the killer, for Zoey at any rate, could not have been taller than five feet eight inches."

"How accurate are those measurements?" Denise asked nervously.

"To within an inch," he replied. "Declan Stevens couldn't have killed her."

Chris tapped a few keys on the computer, bringing up another set of crime scene photos. The one on the left was from Lithia Park where Chloe had been found. On the right was a photo taken from Zoey's dumpsite at the Applegate Lodge bridge.

"Look at these impressions from the drag marks. Notice anything?"

They all studied the images and lightbulbs began flashing in Vince's brain. "They're different depths!"

"Exactly. For Chloe's, it seems like the person who dumped her body was much larger than her, probably a man matching Declan's sizing, so the marks are shallower. Whoever was moving her body wasn't struggling as much."

He paused, using a laser pointer to highlight a certain spot on the image from Zoey's dumpsite. "But here, whoever dropped her body under the bridge was approximately the same size as Zoey. The marks are deeper, and there are more starts and stops in the pattern, meaning they struggled a bit more to move the body from their vehicle to where you found her."

"No. No fucking way in hell! She wouldn't have!" Vince cried, sinking to his knees as realization hit him like a wrecking ball.

There was only one conclusion they could draw from these two bits of information: Audrey had been complicit in the murders. Denise's lavender eyes filled with tears as she clapped a hand over her mouth in shock.

"Oh my God. She played us all, didn't she? How the hell did she do it?" she cried softly.

Sarah lightly cleared her throat, looking at the

report another criminalist had just handed her. "Um..."

"Spit it out, Sarah," Vince groaned, forcing himself to rise from the floor. "Today's not really the day for an 'um,' you know."

"What kind of car does Audrey drive again?"

Vince arched a brow at her, wondering why she was asking. "A 2004 Land Cruiser. Why?"

Pointing to the report in her hand, she continued in a shaking voice. "We found tire tracks matching an early two thousands Land Cruiser at the drop site for Zoey's body."

The blood drained from Vince's face. He thought back to the night Zoey's body had been dumped, and who had been at his place just hours before. Colin had joined them quietly, Ellsie sitting in the bullpen with Angela, a worried expression on their faces.

"She had the body with her..."

"What? What are you talking about?" Colin asked.

"The day Zoey was murdered, Audrey stayed home. But she came over to my place that evening around eight for a beer. She left right after we got the messages from the killer. The lodge is forty-five min-utes away. She had Zoey's body in her damn car when she was at my place, and then drove to dump her."

"Oh my God," Sarah murmured, tears swimming in her eyes.

"Vince," Colin said, placing a hand on his shoulder, "there was no way you could have known. She had all of us fooled."

"She's a cop... she vowed to protect people," he muttered. "I don't understand how she could have any part of this."

"Let's just focus on finding Bridget for now, and arresting Audrey and Declan, okay?" Colin answered.

Nodding miserably, Vince took a deep, shuddering breath. He walked out into the bullpen to find Roger had joined Angela and Ellsie, and was offering the latter a cup of coffee. Her green eyes shot daggers at him as he approached, but he brushed the animosity aside.

"Roger, I need you to stay here with Ellsie and make certain she doesn't leave until we've arrested our suspects, okay?"

"Suspects?" Anderson asked. "As in, more than one?"

"Yeah, sadly it looks like we're dealing with two potential killers here, and I don't want her getting caught in the crossfire," Vince told him.

"I'm quite capable—" Ellsie began, only to be interrupted by a seething Vince.

"Of what? Getting yourself into trouble? I'm very aware of that fact, Ellsie!" Angela gasped at his harsh words as he turned back to Roger. "If she gives you any trouble or tries to leave this building, lock her back in the holding cell for obstruction, okay?"

Mouth agape, Ellsie leapt from her chair to try and slap him, but he caught her wrist in midair. "Wrong move, baby," he growled in her ear. Meeting the shocked eyes of Roger, he nodded for the man to follow him as he dragged her back toward the cells once more.

She kicked and screamed the entire way, attempting to fight his vise-like hold on her wrist, but Vince was done dealing with her shit. With Roger's help, he tossed her back into the cell she had just vacated and locked the door. He dropped the keys into the other man's hand and walked away, never looking back.

⎯⎯•⎯⎯

6:32 p.m.

Colin, Angela, Sarah, and Vince arrived at the Stevens home, finding the windows dark. Dusk had long since passed, lengthening the shadows that ominously followed them as they silently approached the building, weapons drawn. Finding the door locked, Colin pulled out a lock-picking kit from his pocket and set to work while the others watched his back. Once the door sprung open, Colin replaced his kit and drew his gun, and they all stepped inside the home.

Sparse didn't even begin to describe the place. It was evident that Audrey and Declan had begun packing and moving out long before she announced that intention to the department. There was little furniture remaining and no personal effects anywhere. The four officers stuck together as they swept the house, looking for their suspects and their final victim.

"There's no one here," Sarah whispered, as they stood in the back hall.

Her feet were resting on a black and red rug, running the length and breadth of the space. As she went to take a step forward, the boards under her feet emitted the slightest groan. All eyes swiveled to where she stood, questions pricking at the back of their minds. Colin gestured for Sarah to quietly move closer to him as Vince knelt down to peer under the rug.

"There's a fucking trap door under here!" Vince hissed in surprise. "You have got to be kidding me!"

Together, he and Colin finished rolling the rug out of the way before turning their attention to the well-concealed portal in the floor. While Colin held his gun level with the entrance, Vince slowly raised the door to have it lean against the wall, revealing a dark passageway running beneath the house. Stone steps descended into the gloomy basement, a strong musty odor wafting upward.

Vince went first, the girls following and Colin bringing up the rear as they entered the bowels of the earth. Stone and dirt made up the floor, and a handful of hanging lights illuminated their path. Shadows seemed to reach for them as they continued on, like silent curling fingers trying to ensnare them. The eerie dungeon-like basement seemed to go on for miles, like a sick Halloween fun house.

The group found the cell where Chloe and Zoey had been held, the hook still suspended from the ceiling. The noose was in the corner, tossed like a forgotten ragdoll. Across the way, a small room housed raised beds filled with plants sporting purplish-blue flowers and grow lights for the sinister wolfsbane nursery Audrey and Declan had grown.

On and on they went, finding rooms with heinous tools like knives, guns, and bondage equipment. Another held computers, a 3D printer, cameras, and more. Vince hit a key on the computer and the screen illuminated, the unaltered video of Declan kissing Chloe cued up.

"Good thing Chloe is such a fucking lightweight, huh, Declan?" came Audrey's voice.

"She made it easy to put the GHB in her drink, that's for sure," Declan agreed as he pulled off Chloe's skirt. "Is David still out?"

"I'm not an amateur, baby," Audrey sneered. "Of course, he's out. And tomorrow, when they find themselves naked in their own bed, they'll think they fucked each other."

Chloe was now lying completely nude on the bed. Declan held out his hand to Audrey behind the camera. "Wanna get in on this, honey?" he said with a seductive wink.

"I'm going to go make sure David doesn't puke in his sleep. Just go on and fuck her as many times as you want, but make sure you're done in five hours. I want them back home before six a.m.," she answered.

"And you're sure she didn't lie about being primed?"

"Oh, for fuck's sake, Declan! Yes, she went as far as showing me her damn ovulation test! She's at the perfect

time of the month to get pregnant, and I know for a fact Elijah is sterile, so it's not like he helped her the other day. Now, put your fucking dick in her and do your job! She has to get pregnant for this to work correctly!"

"Relax, baby. I'll take care of it."

"Sorry I snapped," Audrey said quietly. "I just really want this to go smoothly so we can put the plan in motion."

Declan kissed her forehead. "And it will. It just works in our favor that Chloe's always had a thing for me and trusts you without question. I think she would be on that bed with me even without the drugs making her more compliant."

"Believe me, Declan, she would. Now, take care of her and then you can play with me when this is over," she told him as she turned away.

The sounds of her retreating steps echoed on the recording as Declan turned to his unsuspecting victim. Chloe's eyes were glazed as he approached her, like a demon from hell. It didn't take long, though. until Declan was causing her to moan in pleasure, the effects of the drugs they gave her ensuring she wouldn't complain.

"Oh God, turn it off," Sarah whimpered.

Vince obliged, the bile rising in his stomach. He had thought the sickest part of this was that Audrey had been involved in the murders, but knowing she had deliberately drugged her best friend so Declan could rape to get her pregnant, and then planned her murder, was despicable. Shuddering, they all turned away from the computers and headed back into the dimly lit hallway.

Coming to the end of the basement at last, they found a room with only a dirt floor. A freshly turned dirt floor. With shovels thrown to one side.

"Holy shit!" Vince yelled. "Bridget must be under here!"

Colin and Vince quickly holstered their weapons and began digging. Angela whipped out her cell phone, amazed she was able to get a signal. She called for an ambulance to come to their location as the men continued to chip away at the dirt. After a few moments, they hit a wooden box.

Prying up the lid, they found Bridget inside, still. They lifted her out of her intended coffin, and carefully pulled the tape from her mouth. Colin felt the side of her neck, relived to find a pulse. Her eyes slowly fluttered open, fear making them wide.

"No! I—" she flailed, terror spiking in her voice.

"It's okay, Bridget," Vince soothed. "You're safe now."

"No, no, no," she cried.

"Bridget," Angela said softly, "we need to know for certain who did this to you."

Mascara smudged and ran down her face grotesquely as she wept. She tried opening her mouth to speak, but no words came forth.

"Was it Audrey and Declan?" Vince asked.

She nodded, crying harder. They heard the sound of approaching sirens, signaling the arrival of the paramedics. Colin and Vince carried her out of the basement to meet them, meeting the shocked faces of Cathy and Henry as they took in the sight. As the two began loading Bridget into the ambulance, Vince's phone vibrated on his hip.

"Cortenza," he answered.

"Vince, it's Anderson. You need to get to downtown now," the other man informed him. "Ellsie just received a call from a girl named Alyce. Somehow I guess she managed to text her something about needing to know the location of Audrey and Declan Stevens."

Fucking hell, Ellsie, Vince thought in annoyance.

"Anyway, this Alyce chick said that they were downtown at Blue Marina, the restaurant at the corner of Elm and Main."

"Thanks, Roger."

Vince hung up and looked at Colin. "We've got to move. Now," he told him.

"I'll stay with Bridget to take her statement once she's stable," Angela informed them.

"Lawson? Are you up for this?" Vince asked.

Sarah swallowed hard and threw back her shoulders. Chewing on her bottom lip, she nodded in the affirmative and followed Colin and Vince to the car.

———•———

7:49 p.m.

Colin had phoned the restaurant once they had left the house, telling the manager not to allow the Stevenses to leave. Uncertain, the manager finally agreed, and the three officers sped back into town. When they arrived, they could see Audrey and Declan sitting at the back of the restaurant, laughing and drinking. Vince felt his blood beginning to boil at the sight.

Walking in, they waited as long as possible before making their presence known to the two killers in their midst. Declan spotted them first, a look of surprise lighting in his icy blue eyes. Audrey noticed his expression and turned her blonde head to find them approaching, hands all on the weapons at their sides.

"Vince? What's going on?" she asked innocently.

"Drop the act, Audrey," he hissed. "We found Bridget. We found the basement and the videos. We know what you two did."

"Do you now?" Declan purred.

"Declan, I would suggest you shut the fuck up—"

"Feeling bitter, are we, Vince?" he interrupted. "What's the matter? Afraid I fucked Ellsie better than you?"

Audrey smirked at Vince's glowering face as her husband continued to taunt her partner. Vince felt the disgust growing in the pit of his stomach as the cold smile reached her eyes. How could he have been so blind for so damn long to not realize she was a sociopath?

"Let's not make this any harder than it needs to be," Colin told them. "Stand up slowly and keep your hands where we can see them."

"You want to see our hands?" came the deep, sinister reply. Declan slowly rose from the table, his arms crossed as he tried to reach into his jacket.

"Hands where we can see them, asshole!" Vince ordered, his eyes narrowing on Declan.

Audrey remained seated, her sexy red dress seeming to grow shorter the longer she sat. Sarah whipped her gun from the holster, along with Colin and Vince, and trained the weapon on Declan.

"Hands up!" she barked, doing her best to sound fearless.

"You sure you want me to do that, cutie?" Declan taunted. "You're looking a little shaky there, Sarah. Do you need me to come over and hold you?"

"Wow, Audrey, you're really going to let your husband talk to another woman like that?" Vince asked distastefully.

She chuckled, the sound low and primal. "What can I say? I like a man who can take charge."

"There's a difference between taking charge and being a sadistic bastard. He is definitely the latter," he announced. Vince cocked his head to one side and continued angrily. "And to think I thought I knew you. We've been partners for five damn years!"

Audrey's blue eyes lit with contempt as she stared back at him. "And that is precisely why you never figured out anything, Cortenza. You thought you could pigeon-hole me just like everyone else. Well...guess again," she shrugged.

"We did think about inviting you to join us, Vince, but you're just too damn noble for your own good." Declan eyed Sarah wolfishly. "Now, you sweetness, would be fun to break."

Sarah narrowed her eyes at him, disgusted by the words escaping his mouth. Beside her, she could feel Vince bristling as well. A sudden motion caught her attention, as Declan began pulling a gun from his jacket.

"Drop it!" she cried.

A sinister smile turned his mouth upward as he continued to taunt her with the weapon. Gasps from the other patrons in the restaurant filled her ears, and Sarah looked him square in the eye before she pulled the trigger.

The first shot hit his arm, causing the gun he'd been holding to drop to the ground. A roar of primal rage burst from his lips and he lunged forward. She fired again, catching him squarely in the chest amidst the screams of running dinner guests.

"Declan!" Audrey shrieked, watching the blood blossom on his chest. "You little—"

Her words cut off as she revealed the gun she had strapped to her thigh, the sights trained on Sarah. She managed three rapid shots before Colin and

Vince fired their own weapons, hitting her several times in the chest. As the blood dribbled from her mouth, Audrey collapsed atop Declan's still form.

Colin kept his gun trained on the two of them as Vince turned to Sarah. Shock registered in his brain the instant before she fell. He barely managed to catch her before her head hit the floor, her breathing wheezing gasps.

"Vince," she whispered, pain lacing her weak voice.

"Hang in there, Lawson!" he ordered, putting pressure on her bullet-riddled chest.

Her hazel eyes began to glaze over, and the light was rapidly diminishing. Vince held her closer, listening as the manager was calling for the ambulance. Sirens were heard in the distance, Colin having already called for back-up on the way.

"Hear that, Sarah? Help is on the way. Just... hang on," Vince urged.

"I... I don't think..." her voice trailed.

"Sarah!" he cried, gently slapping her cheek to try and wake up her up.

The light in her eyes died completely, and her final breath shuddered from her lungs. The hand that had gripped his arm slipped and lay still against the floor. Vince struggled against the weight threatening to crush his chest as she died in his arms.

EPILOGUE

One year later...

The night that the Dice Killers were finally stopped haunted everyone involved in the case. The notion that a cop and her husband had brutally and maliciously murdered so many was no easy task to forget.

Vince took several months off to deal with the trauma from having to fire on his partner and then holding Sarah's body in his arms as she died. The emotional damage that had occurred as a result of everything that came to light during the course of the investigation formed a wedge between him and Ellsie, one that they found themselves unable to get around.

After weeks of arguments and tears, they decided to part ways. Months later, they were able to meet up for a drink as friends. Now, Vince's playboy days are truly behind him as he has finally settled down and found Giselle Martin, a schoolteacher in Medford. The two are scheduled to marry in six months, while Ellsie is taking time to be by herself and adapt to her new role as assistant editor at the paper.

Shawn Mitchel retired as police chief and is slowly working to get back on his feet. Denise has been helping him through his grief, and rumor has it they have been getting closer. Nothing official yet, but there is definitely something between them.

Bridget and Elijah have officially divorced, and she declined to sue him for everything he had. She's in intense therapy thanks to the trauma Audrey and Declan inflicted upon her. Elijah has been adjusting to life without her and the knowledge that he will never be able to father a child. The information came out of left field when the police were reviewing all the videos the Stevenses had made during their murderous plot.

David Harper sold Chloe's florist shop to Liliana and then moved back east to Chicago. No one has heard from him in almost a year, and no one expects to hear from him ever again. The only connection he had to Ashland is gone, and with her went his motivation for living.

The people of Ashland look back at the events with eerie retrospection, unable to wrap their minds around the diabolical path that Audrey and Declan chose. The way they were able to mastermind the entire situation, the utter lack of remorse, the seeming normalcy that they exuded all lend to the incomprehensible realization that it wasn't a terrifying nightmare. It was a living hell that only ended when the two heinous game players were wiped from the board...

ABOUT THE AUTHOR

While originally planning to work as a zoologist, author Emberlyn Grace has always been captivated by literature. She has been married to her loving husband, Mark, for twelve years, happily homeschools her three children and has a wide range of animals under her care. In her spare time, she enjoys reading, cooking, and spending time with her busy family. Emberlyn's favorite pastime is watching the sun set over the field behind her home in the Midwest.